2/24
HE

CW00741731

Oxfordshire l

To renew:

www.oxfordshire.gov.uk/libraries

or

use the Oxfordshire Libraries app

or

contact any Oxfordshire Library

OXFORDSHIRE
COUNTY COUNCIL

3303850973

A MESSAGE FROM CHICKEN HOUSE

For some reason I always wanted to be a highwayman – it's the masks and horses I expect. So you'll see why I was blown away when Anna sent me this extraordinarily excellent story of a young girl who wields a magical mask that turns her into a brigand for justice! There's also terrific action, tum-tickling comedy and some surprises about who can really save the nation. Stand and deliver! (Well, OK, you can sit down to read.)

BARRY CUNNINGHAM
Publisher
Chicken House

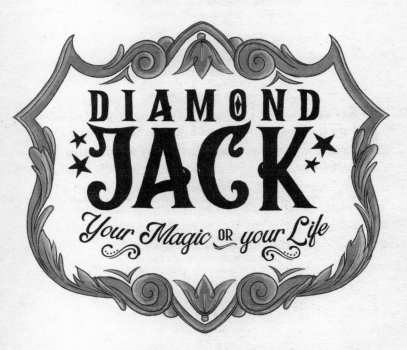

DIAMOND JACK

Your Magic OR your Life

ANNA RAINBOW

2 PALMER STREET, FROME,
SOMERSET BA11 1DS

Text © Anna Waterworth 2024
Cover illustration © Isabelle Follath 2024

First published in Great Britain in 2024
Chicken House
2 Palmer Street
Frome, Somerset BA11 1DS
United Kingdom
www.chickenhousebooks.com

Chicken House/Scholastic Ireland, 89E Lagan Road, Dublin Industrial Estate,
Glasnevin, Dublin D11 HP5F, Republic of Ireland

Cover and interior design by Steve Wells
Cover illustration by Isabelle Follath
Typeset by Dorchester Typesetting Group Ltd
Printed in Great Britain by Clays, Elcograf S.p.A

FSC
www.fsc.org
MIX
Paper | Supporting
responsible forestry
FSC® C018072

1 3 5 7 9 10 8 6 4 2

British Library Cataloguing in Publication data available.

PB ISBN 978-1-913322-72-4
eISBN 978-1-915947-05-5

For Lucy
Dear cousin and dearest friend

CHAPTER 1

All was quiet in Mr Browning's Emporium of Strange and Magical Things when a highwayman burst through the door. His cape swirled like a black sail, his mask was a dark slash across his eyes, and a pair of silver pistols gleamed in his hands.

'Stand and deliver, your money or your life,' he roared.

Mr Browning's granddaughter, Bramble Browning, dropped her waxed polishing-cloth on the counter and jumped. The bell that was mounted above the door continued to sing, drowning out the ragged

hitch of Bramble's breath. Yet as she looked at the outlaw, relief spread through her; the mask was just a strip of black fabric, the guns were merely painted wood, and most importantly, the man behind the mask was not a man at all, but a twelve-year-old boy called Ernest.

Her best friend.

She threw her cloth, smacking him square in the chest. 'Ernest! You scared the life out of me.'

'You got me, Bram. I'm hit. I'm hit.' He stumbled to the ground, grabbing his chest as if he were shot.

Bram rolled her eyes. 'When will you stop with all this highwayman nonsense? Honestly! What if we'd had customers? What if Grandpa had been here?' She winced at how much she sounded like her older sister, Lena, as if fun wasn't allowed. But it was the first time Grandpa had asked Bram to open up shop on her own, and she didn't want to let him down.

Ernest scooped up the cloth and handed it back. His deep brown skin and black curls gleamed in the morning light that slanted through the large arched window.

'Firstly, Gramps loves me.' Ernest straightened his mask. 'I happen to know he thinks my interest in highwaymen is adorable.'

'He thinks it's ridiculous,' Bram muttered.

Grandpa made no secret of the fact he thought highwaymen were villainous thugs, certainly not the celebrities Ernest seemed to think they were. Bram never paid much attention to them either. Why would she care about people who robbed others? Besides, Grandpa refused to have any of the 'Wanted, dead or alive' posters in the shop.

'And secondly,' Ernest said, 'I checked that you were alone through the window. You looked kind of sad.'

'So you thought you'd cheer me up by giving me a heart attack?'

Ignoring her, he twirled around, letting his cape flutter out like the skirt of a dancing girl. 'Do you like it? It's just a petticoat I found in the shop.'

Ernest's ma ran the dressmaker's shop next door. Bram dreaded to think how much trouble he'd be in when she found one of the petticoats missing.

'Yeah, it looks great,' she admitted. He was a dab hand at stitching and fiddling with clothes.

Nipping around the counter to examine the costume more thoroughly, she pulled out the cloak to find the shape of a mask neatly snipped from one of its corners.

She couldn't stop the laughter from bubbling up. 'Does your ma know you've stolen this for your dressing-up box?'

'Dressing-up box?' he said, pretending to be angry. 'Not only am I a highwayman, I'm Diamond Jack, the bravest outlaw in all the land.' He thrust one of his toy guns upwards. 'Stealing from the rich to feed the poor.'

'Stealing from the rich to feed the poor? I don't think that's true.' It was a nice idea, but Bram was pretty sure that outlaw highwaymen kept the loot for themselves.

But Ernest nodded so fiercely his mask slipped. 'It *is* true, Bram, it is! Most highwaymen are only in it to get rich, I agree, but not Diamond Jack. He's a good'un.' He straightened his mask and waved his pistol. 'Sworn to protect the people and the one true queen.'

Bram had heard a rumour that Diamond Jack supported Queen Georgina, although that alone didn't make him a 'good'un' as Ernest claimed. But she dipped into a curtsey anyway.

'All hail, Queen Georgina.'

Playing along felt like the right thing to do, for she supported the young queen. Queen Georgina had sadly fallen ill several years earlier and had since been replaced by her younger sister, Lavinia, the Princess Regent. Bram disliked the Princess Regent. As soon as Queen Georgina had fallen ill and moved to the royal hospital on Rosemary Hill, Lavinia had used her powers to raise the price of food and rent, making the poor even poorer.

The sound of high heels clicking against the stairs caused them both to startle.

'Lena,' Ernest whispered, tucking his toy guns into his belt.

'Let's see how brave you are when my sister's here,' Bram said with a chuckle.

Lena emerged from the door that came from the small flat above the emporium where she and Bramble lived with Grandpa. Lena was sixteen, four years older than Bram, a fact which she loved to remind Bram of. But today, dressed in Mama's favourite velvet gown and a matching pink bonnet that tamed her brown curls, she looked at least twenty. Bram tucked her own hazel ringlets beneath her straw hat, suddenly feeling very young and foolish.

Lena was staying the night with Aunt Jane, who lived in the neighbouring town. She carried a small chatelaine bag with some coins inside. Bram couldn't tell if she'd dabbed a little of Mama's rouge on her cheeks, or if she was simply reddening with annoyance. Her sister also shared Grandpa's dislike for highwaymen.

Just as Bram expected, Lena made a noise that sounded like *humph*. 'I've already told you, Ernest, no highwaymen in the shop.' Her blue eyes flashed.

Bram prickled at her sister's tone – only *she* was allowed to tell Ernest off, he was her friend after all. 'He was just showing me his costume, no harm done.'

'No harm done?' She shoved her hands on her hips. 'Grandpa left you in charge and you're already playing daft games with your friends.'

Guilt nipped at Bram's stomach. Guilt and irritation – it wasn't *her* fault Ernest had turned up looking like this.

'I'm not just any old highwayman,' Ernest said, frowning. 'I'm Diamond Jack, and you can't be mean to Diamond Jack. He's a national treasure.'

Lena's nostrils flared. 'In case you've forgotten, Diamond Jack is dead. He died a year ago.'

'Disappeared, Lena. *Disappeared*,' he said. 'Everyone needs a holiday, even the Diamond. But he'll be back.'

Lena pinched the bridge of her nose as if staving off a headache and said, 'Look, I just don't want any silliness in the emporium. It's a business, not a playground.'

'What? No silliness in this extremely serious place?' Ernest gestured to the walls and shelves. Every surface was cluttered with bizarre knick-knacks. There was a mirror that gifted the gazer extra beauty (it didn't), magic boxes that couldn't be opened (they could) and possessed candles that fizzed and sparked when lit (they really did, but only because Grandpa had sprinkled them with flint).

'Less of the sarcasm,' Lena said. 'Magic is a serious business indeed.'

Ernest scoffed. 'You know that nothing here is actually enchanted, right? *Real* magic is dead. It died out years ago. But do you know who *isn't* dead?' He thumped his chest. 'Diamond Jack!'

Rolling her eyes, Lena switched her attention back to Bram. 'Grandpa won't be long. He had some errands to run this morning, that's all.' Her voice softened as she took Bram's hand. 'I need to catch my train so you'll be on your own for about an hour or so.'

'I know,' Bram replied.

Lena had already told her this about ten times yesterday, and about three times at breakfast. Since their parents died a year ago in a riding accident, Lena had become less of a sister and more of an overprotective governess. Bram knew it was because she cared, but sometimes it felt a little suffocating. The funny thing was, Bram had barely seen Lena before their parents' death. She was always off doing her own thing, whereas now, she was like a second shadow.

'It should be quiet.' Lena gestured outside; but for a few lamp posts and dried-up leaves skittering in the breeze, the street was empty. The shops that tended to get busy, like the butcher's and the baker's, hadn't woken up yet. Their brightly coloured awnings sat like heavy eyelids above their panes.

'I know,' Bram repeated, though she gave Lena's hand a squeeze, not wanting to appear rude.

'I'll be back on the first train tomorrow morning.'

Bram nodded. There are only so many times you can say *I know*, she decided.

Lena wagged a gloved finger at her. 'No closing up shop before Grandpa's home, no playing in the street, no joining in Ernest's silly highwayman games, and absolutely no going in the garden shed. Agreed?'

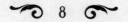

Bram nodded. It was easier to just agree. Lena pulled her into a hug and Bram let the soothing scent of her lavender hair oil fill her nose.

'Bye, Lena,' she said.

As Lena walked from the shop, Ernest threw his arms wide. 'Where's my hug?'

The door slammed, causing the bell to jangle.

Ernest slumped. 'Your sister really doesn't like me, does she?'

'It's just because of your costume.' She sighed. 'And you know what she's like, she worries about every little thing since . . .' Her sentence faded from her lips. She didn't need to say it – they both knew what she was talking about. Her fingers toyed with her necklace, a delicate chain threaded through a silver locket; it had been a gift from her parents and since their death, she hadn't taken it off once. Yet for all her love of it, she hadn't been able to open it. Inside were two miniature paintings of her parents, and she knew that gazing upon their smiling faces would simply be too much to bear.

Just then, Bram felt a strange pulling sensation in her stomach. At first, she thought it was grief, but it was different from anything she'd ever felt before, like a fishing line hooking her belly. She glanced down, scowling.

'Are you OK?' Ernest asked.

'Yeah. Just hungry.' It was a lie, but she didn't want to alarm her friend.

'Have you checked Cornelius this morning?' he asked.

'Not yet.'

'What if Gramps left biscuits?'

'He might have.' She glanced at the stag's head mounted behind the counter. He wasn't a real stag's head, just some soft velveteen fabric topped with wooden antlers. In his mouth, Grandpa used to leave Bram secret notes or scribbled maps telling her where the freshly baked cookies were hidden.

'You can check, if you like,' she said, distracted.

That strange sensation was strengthening, and it seemed to be pulling her towards the kitchen at the back of the shop.

'Not likely,' Ernest muttered. 'He looks like he can still bite.'

Confused but curious, Bram headed to the kitchen. It was exactly as she had left it. Toast crumbs scattered on the table, copper kettle humming on the range, plates piled in the sink waiting to be washed. But still the tugging sensation grew. It was coaxing her towards the back garden, she was sure of it.

'Time for a cuppa already?' Ernest said.

Ignoring him, she crossed to the back door where the sensation swelled until she felt like a fish being reeled in. Was magic at work? But that was impossible, like Ernest said – magic was dead. It had been for centuries.

So what was pulling her?

Her eyes landed on the shed and a feeling of warmth exploded in her tummy and spread throughout her veins.

'Jackpot,' Bram whispered.

'Jackpot?' Ernest said, excited. 'What jackpot?'

'I don't know,' she replied. 'But we're about to find out.'

CHAPTER 2

Bram stepped into the summer's morning and wound her way up the weed-beaten path. The garden was wild and colourful, just like Grandpa.

'Where are we going?' Ernest asked.

'The forbidden shed.'

'Ooh, Bramble.' He wriggled his eyebrows so his mask slipped. 'I like this new you, normally you don't put a foot out of line.'

She wanted to tell him about the strange pulling sensation, the warmth in her veins, but she didn't want

to worry him. Besides, she rather liked the way he was looking at her, like she was the brave and reckless one for once.

The shed was as unkempt as the garden: a squat building of pitted red bricks with a single window caked in moss, and roof tiles that clung on by stubbornness alone. Bram dug around in her apron pocket for Grandpa's loop of keys whilst Ernest skipped on the spot. It didn't take long to find the right key, it was the only one that Bram hadn't used, yet she found herself pausing before unlocking the door.

Whatever was calling to her could be dangerous – it wasn't normal to be drawn to something and Grandpa had always told her to keep clear of the shed. Then another even more terrifying thought occurred to her: what if it wasn't some*thing*, but some*one*?

Centuries ago, before magic was banned, there had been wizards and witches, warlocks and mighty sorcerers. Most were good but some were bad, and the history books said that when the bad ones got too powerful the royal family outlawed all magic. Bram shook the thought from her head. No. Her mild-mannered grandpa would never keep someone locked in a shed, *could* never, especially not a spell-wielding warlock. The idea was simply preposterous.

'Come on, Bram,' Ernest said, lifting her from her thoughts. 'I simply have to know what's inside now.' He pulled his toy pistols from his belt and grinned. 'Maybe Gramps has imprisoned a family of gnomes, stopping them from rampaging through the neighbourhood gardens.'

She laughed, forgetting her worries for a second, and turned the key. The door swung open on its own, as if welcoming her.

The warmth in her veins intensified.

She was close.

Blinking away the dust, she took everything in. The disappointment dropped like a stone through her body. There was nothing of interest, certainly no wizards or witches or gnomes, just a haphazard pile of old boxes that would probably hurt her if they fell. The July sun streamed in from the door, casting their shadows across the junk.

'It's just some old stock.' Ernest sighed. 'I was kind of hoping there'd be gnomes.'

'Me too.'

But Bram's veins were still fizzing with warmth and she needed to get to the bottom of it. And whilst she hated to admit it, disobeying Lena planted a thrill inside her. So she stepped inside and picked her way through the piles of strange and possibly forbidden magical antiquities: pouches of fake gemstones, a box of rabbit paws, a selection of magician's hats.

The fizzing in her veins hadn't stopped. Frustrated, Bram spun in a circle. It could be anything. She'd assumed it would glow or hum as she got closer, but now she was here, the theory seemed as silly as imprisoned wizards. Or gnomes.

Perhaps she'd imagined the whole thing.

She began thumbing through a stack of newspapers, dated in the future, while Ernest shook some jars.

'Let's not disturb anything too much,' she said. 'I don't want Lena to know we've been in here.'

'Diamond Jack is not afraid of your sister,' Ernest said, brandishing his pistols and knocking a shelf of ancient books to the ground. Dust and dead flies landed on his hair.

'Careful.' Bram raised her palms.

But this only spurred him on. Leaping on to a wooden box, he pointed his toy guns at her.

'Stand and deliver, Bramble Browning. Your money or your life. And if you haven't got any money, a couple of ham sandwiches will do.' The box wobbled beneath his boots.

'Ernest! Seriously, be careful.'

'I'll be careful once Queen Georgina is restored to her rightful throne and the wicked Princess Regent is rotting behind bars. Down with Lavinia!' He waved his guns and started jumping. 'Woah!'

He slipped, crashing into the wall behind.

'Ernest!' Bram rushed to his side.

'I'm OK,' he groaned.

He was a muddle of limbs, grime and dust, and a few bricks lay around him.

'That must have hurt,' she said, pulling him to his feet and helping him knock the dirt from his clothes.

'Look, a hidden alcove,' Ernest said, ignoring any pain.

The missing bricks revealed a small nook behind the wall.

Bram's blood fizzed so strongly that she was sure she was made of bubbles alone. This was it. Dropping to her knees, she cleared away some of the debris. Unlike the surrounding wall, these bricks were smooth, the mortar pale and clean. Whatever lurked behind had been put there recently. *Did Grandpa do this?* Bram thought. *Did Lena know about it?* Feeling excluded, she reached inside the hole, telling herself there was nothing to be afraid of – it was just like reaching inside Cornelius's mouth.

Her fingers fell upon something smooth, angular and cool. A box perhaps? It began to vibrate, as if awakening at her touch. Bram knew this should alarm her, but instead she felt strangely calm.

'Jackpot,' she whispered, sliding it out.

It *was* a box. Long and rectangular, like the kind used to store pistols. Galloping horses had been carved around the sides. Intrigued, she wiped the dust from the top to reveal the image of a flying dove inlaid in mother of pearl. The bird was the symbol of the one true queen and had once flown from every golden flag around town and country. But ever since the Princess Regent had taken power, the gold had been replaced by flags of silver with a raven as black as tar stamped in the centre.

'Do you think there are pistols inside?' she whispered, fear in her voice. She'd never seen real guns before. And these guns could be . . . *enchanted*.

'Nah. They wouldn't fit,' Ernest replied. 'Open it,' he urged, unable to contain his excitement.

Her fingers hovered on the metal clasp. She had always been told not to go into the shed, yet she'd disobeyed and found something that clearly wasn't meant to be found. Maybe she should just put it back and pretend it never happened. But the curiosity was overwhelming.

'Oh, for goodness' sake,' Ernest said, swiping the box from her. He threw back the lid before she could complain.

Inside was a small strip of red cloth.

The disappointment was back, this time boulder-sized. She'd assumed it would be something magical, a wand perhaps, or an enchanted treasure map, but this was just a boring piece of fabric.

Yet Ernest's eyes were wide and his mouth opened in a gasp. 'Could it possibly be?'

Bram noticed the intricate stitching, the eyeholes, the tapering of the fabric at each end into two ties. She nodded. 'I think it might be, Ernest.'

'A highwayman's mask.' His voice morphed into a joyful whoop. 'A real one! This isn't any old jackpot – it's a *Diamond* Jack-pot.' He ripped the handmade mask from his face and discarded it amongst the bricks, delight sparkling in his eyes as he smoothed out the scarlet mask so it was ready to wear.

Bram was about to tell him to be careful, about to tell him about the pulling sensation in her stomach and the fizzing in her veins, when a voice split the stale air of the shed.

'Ernest! Where is my petticoat?'

It was his mother. She was shouting over the fence, as she often did when Ernest forgot to do his chores.

His face fell. 'She sounds cross, doesn't she?'

'You get back here right now!' she bellowed.

Bram nodded. She really did.

With a reluctant sigh, he laid the mask back in the box and handed it to her. 'I better go.'

Bram caught his cloak as he stood to leave. 'Ernest, wait, I have to tell you something.'

'Ernest Kassongo!' his ma shouted.

'She only uses my full name when I'm in real trouble. Sorry, Bram, I'll be back later – if I'm allowed. Don't do anything cool without me.' He picked up his fake pistols and bolted from the shed.

Bram suddenly felt very alone.

Turning her attention back to the scarlet mask in the box, she whispered, 'Was it you pulling at my tummy?'

She picked the mask up. Instantly, it made her fingers tingle, almost like the dull ache of a nettle sting. It had called to her, she was sure of it. But *how* had it called to her?

It had to be magic.

She swallowed. She desperately wanted to try it on, but it was too dangerous. Magic had been banned for a reason. Bram decided to put it back in the box, replace the bricks, and forget all about it. Maybe she'd pluck up the courage to ask Grandpa about it someday.

Yet no matter how hard she tried, she couldn't put the mask down. It was as though it were stuck to her skin. She tried shaking her hands, tried pumping them open and closed, but nothing seemed to work. Then, without her permission, her arms began moving, lifting the material towards her face; the mask was somehow dragging her hands upwards. Panic exploded in her chest as she fought the urge, but it was as if the mask wanted to be worn. Before she knew it, she'd pulled the fabric over her eyes and tied the ends at the back of her head.

An unfamiliar whooshing sensation travelled through her body. The fizzing was back. The skin around her eyes grew hot and itchy.

Then ... nothing.

She started to laugh.

What had she expected? It was just a mask. Of course it hadn't stuck to her fingers. Of course she hadn't felt a hook in her tummy. The dark, creepy shed was playing tricks on her. Magic was dead.

'Stand and deliver, your money or your life,' she whispered, then chuckled as she untied the fabric.

But the mask wasn't going anywhere.

It was well and truly stuck.

CHAPTER
3

'For the love of Queen Georgina!'

She started tugging, harder and harder. She had to get the mask off before Grandpa came home, and she couldn't very well serve the customers dressed as a robber. And if the mask was enchanted, what was it capable of? Worse – what was *she* capable of when she was wearing it? If it could make her hands move, what else could it make her do? Panic rose up Bram's throat like magma from a volcano.

She tried to ease her fingers under the edge where the material met her skin, but it was as if the mask was welded on. Crossing the garden, she sprinted to the house, pulling at the pesky red fabric all the way. Thankfully, the shop remained empty, though the street outside was growing busier.

She needed help. She couldn't wait for Lena or Grandpa, so it had to be Ernest. She raced to the shop door to change the open sign. Through the window, she spied a man with a pointed face like a weasel's. When he saw her, his face lit up as though he recognized her, even though Bram was sure she'd never met him before. She offered him an awkward smile and watched as he scurried off into the crowd, rubbing his hands together in glee.

Just when she thought the day couldn't get any weirder, the mask came free.

She was so shocked that she pushed it back to her face to see if it stuck again. Thankfully, it came away just fine. Had she dreamt it all? No way. Only minutes before, that mask had been a magnet.

Confused, she bundled the scarlet material inside her apron, just as the shop bell rang.

Grandpa.

She was so relieved to see him, she wrapped her hands around his middle and squeezed until he groaned. The layers of his clothing sank beneath her grip and she was reminded of how slim he was – all elbows, spindly limbs and sharp angles, though his smile was the softest she'd ever seen.

'Are you OK?' he asked. 'You look a little pale.'

'I'm fine, thanks.' She knew she should tell him about the mask, she just didn't know how.

He dropped a kiss on her head and bounced behind the counter to hang up his jacket with quick, nimble hands. He always looked like he was dancing, Bram decided, his feet and head moving as if he could hear music no one else could.

'Did you check Cornelius?' he asked. 'I left a note, same place as always.'

'No, sorry, I didn't get round to it.'

'So you didn't find the scones?'

She shook her head.

'No matter,' he said, patting Cornelius on his velveteen muzzle. 'It's always scone o'clock in the emporium. I'll stick the kettle on in a mo.'

Same as always, he ignored the grandfather clock and checked his pocket watch, which was one of his most treasured possessions, with a thick gold chain and a pale clock face engraved with flying doves, the symbol of Queen Georgina. He once told Bram he'd won it in a card game, though Bram couldn't imagine Grandpa ever going out to grimy taverns and doing such things.

'And everything's run smoothly?' he said. 'No fires, no robberies, no lawyers?' He winked.

'No, but Grandpa—' She was about to tell him about the mask, but he cut over her.

'Well done, Bramble. I'm so proud of you. You've really matured in the past year. I know it hasn't been easy but I was wrong not to trust you sooner.'

Bram couldn't listen to his kind words any longer. 'I'm so sorry, Grandpa, I went into the forbidden shed. I knew I shouldn't, but I got this strange feeling in my tummy like something was pulling me, which I know sounds strange, but when we got there, we knocked into the wall and there were bricks and dead bugs' – she flung her hands around, miming falling stones and exploding dust clouds – 'and then we found a small box, and I didn't want to open it in case there were real-life guns inside, but Ernest said it was too small for real-life guns and then' – she paused for breath – 'I found this.' She pulled the mask from her pocket.

Grandpa went from bemused to statue-still, his bright blue eyes wide with fear. She'd expected him to chuckle and tell her it didn't matter, but instead his mouth opened and his eyebrows shot up. A dark cloud passed over the sapphire of his eyes.

In one sudden movement, he snatched the mask from her fingers and rammed it inside his waistcoat. 'Did anyone see? Anyone except Ernest?' His voice was sharp and wavery all at once.

'No, Grandpa. What's wrong?'

He gripped her shoulders, not hard enough to hurt, but hard enough to fix her to the spot while his stormy eyes bore down on her. 'Are you absolutely positive, Bramble? Think. It's important.'

'Yes, I'm sure.' Best not to mention the weasel-faced man she'd smiled at, as Grandpa looked scared enough as it was.

Finally, his face started dancing again and a laugh barrelled out of him; he was back to being Grandpa. 'Sorry, dear heart. It's fine, it's fine. I didn't mean to scare you.' He started tidying the counter, even though it was already tidy. 'Let's have those scones and I'll tell you about my morning.'

She was about to ask more about the mask when a

dark shadow fell across the shop window. She squinted. Three burly figures were stomping towards the door. Grandpa must have noticed too because his face flickered with anxiety.

Quickly, he opened the tiny cupboard beneath the counter. 'Get inside. And don't come out till they've gone, no matter what.'

Something about his voice made her obey without question. Clambering into the cupboard, she hugged her knees to her body so Grandpa could close her inside.

Moments later, the shop bell chimed.

Her stomach clenched. Grandpa was clearly terrified of the figures outside, and now they were in the shop. Sweat pricked her neck. Her mouth was dry and sour. And as the bell faded, all she could hear was the rush of her own blood in her ears.

It was entirely dark but for a vein of light coming from the join between two wooden panels, so she pressed her eye to it, trying to steady her breath. She could only see one of the men. He was too tall for his clothes, too tall for the shop, his broad shoulders and muscular arms straining against his patched velvet jacket. But it wasn't his size that made him so intimidating, it was his face: so gaunt it looked as though his skin had been stretched over his skull. No muscles, no fat. Just bones, eye sockets and thin, pale lips. She shuddered. He looked familiar, though she couldn't think why.

Squinting, she noticed that his coat was held fast by a row of silver buttons, each engraved with a raven. Were these Princess Lavinia's men?

Grandpa spoke first. 'And what can I do for you?' His voice was surprisingly friendly, as though serving any other customer.

The skull-faced man didn't reply. Rather, it was a woman who spoke, stepping into Bram's line of sight.

'Do you know why we're here, old man?'

Compared to Skull-face, she was thin, birch-like, with a hard face that sat in shadow beneath a triangular hat. A blonde plait roped over her shoulder, and a long dark jacket brushed the tops of mud-speckled boots. She too wore a line of silver raven-clad buttons on her coat. Bram couldn't help but wonder what the Princess Regent wanted with Grandpa.

'Are you here to browse my splendid wares?' Grandpa replied smoothly.

'Not exactly.' She opened her coat, revealing a belt slung diagonally across her chest, hung with blades of every size.

Bram clamped a hand over her mouth to smother a gasp.

The third figure spoke. 'Just hand him over and there won't be any trouble.'

Bram was glad she couldn't see him. His voice was scary enough, filled with gravel and too much salt.

The woman laughed. 'Well, maybe just a *little* trouble.'

The invisible man laughed too – a deep, barking sound.

Skull-face remained quiet and still, reminding Bram of a viper before it strikes.

'Hand who over?' Grandpa said.

'It's like that, is it?' The woman ran her thumb down the bronze handle of one of her daggers.

When Grandpa spoke, his voice was cool. Not an ounce of fear. 'Yes. It's like that.'

Could he not see the bunting of knives draped round the woman's chest, or the huge man with the skull face? Why didn't he escape out the back?

Run, Grandpa, run, Bram wanted to scream, but terror had fused her lips together.

The woman turned to Skull-face. 'Boss?'

Finally, Skull-face moved, his face jerking into a smile. Mean lips pulled back to show even meaner teeth, each one sharp and yellow. 'Tear this place apart,' he growled.

CHAPTER 4

It sounded like an earthquake – crashing, thumping, slamming. Only the whoops of the three villains reminded Bram that this was in fact an attack. She hid inside the cupboard, trying to block out the terrible noises, worrying so much about Grandpa she thought she might be sick, yet feeling so afraid she simply couldn't move.

Tears streamed down her cheeks as the light from the crack flickered from the attack on their home. More banging, more smashing, then the sound of boots coming down the stairs; one of the thugs must have slipped away to check the bedrooms. It made her head pound thinking about those foul beasts touching her things.

'He ain't up there,' the woman said.

'He ain't down here either,' the invisible man said.

Skull-face roared with frustration. 'Fine. Then we take the old man. He might remember something after a few nights in the lair.'

The words were a punch to the guts.

Don't take Grandpa, she tried to scream, but the plea was trapped inside her head. *Please don't take Grandpa.*

She heard a scuffle, a thud on the countertop accompanied by a soft grunt, then the heavy tread of boots. The shop bell chimed.

No.

The door slammed.

No, no, no.

There was not a sound.

It took a moment before Bram could move again. She pushed her eye against the crack.

The three figures had gone. So had Grandpa.

She emerged from her hideout, hiccupping with tears. She needed to get help, needed to rescue

Grandpa, but seeing the ruined emporium caused her to falter. Shelves lay on top of each other like giant toppled dominoes and Grandpa's beloved stock was scattered across the floor – a blanket of trinkets, splintered wood and broken glass. The familiar scent of herbs and incense had been replaced by the tang of body odour and the faint smell of mud.

There was a smudge of blood on the side of the counter.

'Grandpa,' she whispered as she recalled the thudding noise only moments ago.

Refocusing, she scrambled over the chaos and burst from the emporium, heading straight across the street to the butcher's shop. Mr Kipling, the butcher, would help. He was a kind man, who always held back the bacon rind for Bram to fry up with her morning eggs.

She found him slicing lamb chops in the back and quickly told him what had happened. He'd missed the ruckus entirely, and when he saw Grandpa's shop, all the pink drained from his face.

'Goodness.' His voice trembled as he pushed his white hair from his eyes. 'Poor Mr Browning. What a terrible business.'

'There was blood on the counter,' Bram said, wiping her nose with her sleeve.

'You better stay with me. We'll find Mr Wren, he'll be doing his rounds now.'

Mr Wren was the local bobby. Bram always thought his name was rather fitting because like a bird, he was easily startled, always ready to take flight. Just what you didn't want in a law enforcer.

As Bram followed Mr Kipling down the street, the world took on a hazy quality; the trundle of carriages and clicks of hooves seemed so far away. Her mind had gone back to the day her parents died. Of the police coming to their little cottage, and telling her and Lena about the riding accident. Of how nothing felt real, even when Grandpa arrived and took them back to the emporium to live. Tears burnt her eyes – she couldn't lose him too. She just couldn't.

They found Mr Wren sitting on a bench in the park, feeding a swarm of pigeons.

He spotted them running towards him and frowned. 'I'm eating my mid-morning snack. Can't it wait?' The pigeons scattered in a whirl of feathers and he groaned. 'And now you've scared the birds.'

'Mr Wren, come quick,' Mr Kipling said. 'There's

been a kidnapping. Three rogues have taken Mr Browning and ransacked the emporium.'

The policeman seemed unmoved by this, but followed Bram and a very angry Mr Kipling back to Grandpa's shop. Bram's head was still fuzzy with shock, but something about seeing the crime scene again cleared her head. How dare those scoundrels steal her darling grandpa. They needed to be caught. Punished. She burst into action, telling Mr Wren everything she could remember, starting with the cupboard and ending with the abduction.

Mr Wren studied the fallen shelves with a frown. 'It looks like a robbery gone wrong.'

Bram exchanged a frustrated glance with Mr Kipling. 'A robbery?' she said. 'But they didn't steal anything, except for Grandpa.' She knew they hadn't taken any coins, because all the cash was kept in a slim drawer below the counter, right above the cupboard in which she'd crouched.

Mr Wren stroked his chin in small juddery motions. 'Maybe he's trying to stop them. Maybe he's still chasing them now.'

'But they said they were taking him,' she said, frustration creeping into her voice. 'I heard them.

They weren't here to rob us, they were looking for someone.'

The policeman straightened up and shook his head. 'And you're sure he's not chasing them?'

Mr Kipling cleared his throat. 'With all respect, Mr Wren, Bram's grandpa is in his seventies.'

'And there were three of them,' Bram said. 'One of them was carrying knives.'

Mr Wren stared at her.

Bram stared back, defiant.

Eventually, he said, 'I'll go and get back-up. That's what I'll do.'

Bram and Mr Kipling watched him leave. The chirp of the bell now made her stomach lurch.

'They'll find him,' Mr Kipling said. 'Where's your sister?'

'Visiting our aunt. She isn't back till tomorrow morning.'

'You can stay at my house tonight, just in case the scoundrels come back. Mrs Kipling will make you her famous sponge cake, she does make exceedingly good cakes.'

'Thank you, but I'm sure I can stay with Ernest and his ma. I'll go and get him now.'

'Well, you know where I am,' he said.

She nodded gratefully.

Once alone again, Bram took in what had once been the emporium. Who were those awful crooks and who were they looking for? She'd never seen Grandpa look so scared. She swallowed. Yes, she had. Just moments before, when she'd shown him the highwayman's mask. Was it all linked?

Choking back a sob, she began tidying the counter. The stain of blood made her heart sting. Poor Grandpa. At least they'd said something about keeping him a couple of nights, which meant they weren't about to kill him. Yet.

Her hands shook and her tears spotted the wood, but she knew how much Grandpa liked a tidy worktop. *He'll be home soon*, she told herself, *as soon as some proper bobbies arrive and track him down.* She mopped an ink spill, popped his quill back in its pot and returned the biscuit tin to the cupboard. Then, something snagged in her stomach. That strange hooking sensation was back.

Her adrenalin spiked and she followed the direction of the pull, turning around so that she faced the wall where the stag's head was mounted.

'Cornelius!'

She shoved her fingers inside his velvety muzzle; they bumped up against something silky and out of place. A static shock travelled up her hand. The scarlet mask. Grandpa must have stuffed it there so Skull-face and his friends didn't find it.

Slowly, with trembling fingers, she pulled it free, and another question surfaced in her mind: *Did Grandpa hide the mask in Cornelius so Skull-face wouldn't find it, or so I would?*

CHAPTER
5

Once again, Bram's mind lost control of her hands and, no matter how hard she resisted, she couldn't help but tie the mask around her head. The same whooshing sensation sped through her body, the fizzing filled her veins, and even though she was anxious she felt strangely happy. She *knew* she hadn't imagined it.

Just then, the shop bell announced the return of Mr Wren. 'OK then, Bramble, some of my colleagues are on their way—' He looked up, and as his eyes fell on her, he stopped mid-sentence and swallowed down a warbly screech.

He paused. His face turned red.

'Mr Wren?' she said.

The sound of his name jolted him from his daze.

'Gah!' he shouted, before darting from the door and running down the street.

Gah? Quickly, she followed Mr Wren from the shop, assuming he'd spied some vital clue that would cast light on Grandpa's situation or was getting his colleagues.

'Mr Wren,' she shouted. 'Mr Wren, what is it?'

She didn't think it was possible, for he was already running at speed, but he got faster as she called to him.

The street was much busier now, yet silence fell upon it like a snuffed-out candle. Bram glanced around and realized that everyone was staring at her.

'Hello?' she said, more a question than a greeting.

It was as if she were a greedy cat leaping into a crowd of rats. People scurried this way and that, some terrified, others pointing at her with excited grins on their faces. A small boy dashed towards her, asking for her autograph, but his mother hauled him away before he could get too close. And before Bram could make sense of any of it, the street was clear and she stood alone.

What's happening? she thought.

Had the three scoundrels returned? No. The pedestrians had been running from *her*. She looked down – same cotton dress, same apron, same leather shoes – then she touched her face. Apart from the mask, everything was as it should be. Eyes, nose, mouth. Not a monster in sight.

'Was it something I said?' she whispered. Even her voice was ordinary.

Across the road, Mr Kipling stood in his shop behind the glass counter filled with cuts of meat, and even he was gawping at her, yet when their eyes met, he ducked from view. That's when she noticed her reflection in the windowpane. She looked different somehow. Taller. Larger.

Baffled, she went back inside the emporium to find a mirror. The enchanted looking glass that had previously hung proudly on the wall now lay on the floor. She grabbed it. A large crack marred the frame and some of the glass at the edges had splintered, but the face staring back at her was crystal clear.

And it wasn't hers.

CHAPTER
6

Looking back at Bram was the face of a highway-man: a fully grown man with brown eyes the exact colour of her own peering from behind the scarlet mask. An unexpected scream burst from her mouth and she hurled the mirror away to escape the alarming sight.

Her pulse raced and her ears hummed with anxiety. 'What on earth?' she whispered.

Then, slowly, as if reaching towards an injured animal that might bite or scratch, she plucked the mirror from the floor.

The highwayman was still there, staring back from the silver pane. She nodded her head, and so did her reflection. She blinked, coughed, stuck out her tongue, and so did he. Finally, she tapped on the glass and the finger that came tip to tip with her own was that of a man.

Maybe the mirror really is magic. But she knew there was no other reason why Mr Wren and the pedestrians had fled from her. Even so, she left the looking glass in the scrum of shelves and raced upstairs to double-check. Panic made her desperate.

The full-length mirror mounted on the wardrobe of her and Lena's room confirmed what she already knew.

She was a highwayman. A *real* highwayman. And oddly familiar at that.

Her reflection was tall, broad and wore a fitted navy jacket over a frilly white shirt. The coat was fastened by three gold buttons, each engraved with the symbol of the one true queen: a dove in flight. Bram's mind spun back to the villains who stole Grandpa. Was it a coincidence that their jackets were fastened with the Princess Regent's silver buttons? Returning her attention to the mirror, she noticed that the highwayman's trousers and leather boots were flecked with mud, giving the illusion she'd just been riding across the moor. She grasped her cheeks in shock, causing the blue sleeves to fall back and reveal two thick arms dappled with black hair.

Nerves wheeling in her stomach, Bram looked down and checked her actual body. Dress, apron, slender arms covered in fine pale hairs, and where she still held her cheeks, they felt soft and stubble-free. They felt like *her* cheeks. She tousled the ringlets on her head, which felt as they always did – curly and long. Her reflection's hair was dark, floppy and parted in the centre so it resembled the ears of a spaniel.

Only one thing in the mirror matched reality: the scarlet mask.

It was just a glamour.

Relief flooded her, cooling her hot, sweat-drenched skin and settling the fire inside. Grandpa had always been fascinated by magic of the past – hardly surprising considering he owned the emporium – and was always telling Bram about the different kinds of magic. He'd once explained that a glamour was a spell that only made you *appear* to be something. So although her reflection and the onlookers' reactions said otherwise, Bramble was still Bramble. Thank goodness. The thought of transforming into someone else entirely filled her with dread. Who knew how that worked. What if she forgot her true self? What if she forgot her parents? A glamour was much better.

Excitement rippled in her stomach. Her whole life, she'd believed magic to be dead – everyone believed magic to be dead.

And yet here she was, looking like a highwayman.

Something clicked into place. The mask could be why the three thugs turned up. That weaselly-looking man had seen her wearing it after all, or more to the point, he'd seen a dastardly highwayman standing in the shop. What if he'd told someone?

Looking at her new reflection, she noticed a flash of metal around the highwayman's throat. The man in the mirror was wearing the silver locket her parents had given her. *How strange that this one object should somehow shine through the glamour*, she thought.

Before she could make sense of it, a voice called out. 'Miss Browning? It's the police. Are you up there?'

She tugged at the mask, and much to her surprise it came away in one easy action. The highwayman in the mirror transformed back into a twelve-year-old girl.

Thank goodness for that. If the police had seen her like this, she'd have been marched to jail and ended up swinging from a rope.

'Coming,' she called, stuffing the mask into her apron.

Downstairs, Mr Wren stood by the door, his jaw straining and the tendons on his neck standing out. Two more officers, a man and a woman, milled about the shop.

Upon seeing her, the woman rushed over. She was pale-skinned, with a kind face and black hair swept back into a bun. 'Oh, thank goodness you're OK. We were so worried when we heard the reports. My name's Nancy and this is—'

The man who wasn't Mr Wren cut over her. 'Where's he gone?' He pulled his truncheon from his belt and scanned the room with suspicious eyes. They were the brightest of green, and his hair, the colour and texture of straw, sat upon his broad head like thatching. 'Where's Diamond Jack?'

'Diamond Jack?' Bram said, her voice cracking with surprise.

Nancy nodded. 'That's right. Mr Wren said he was here, right in this very shop, and we've had several witnesses come forward to confirm the sighting.' She took Bram by the upper arms and squeezed. 'Did you see him? Is he here?'

Bram couldn't tell if Nancy was excited or scared. Perhaps both.

No wonder I recognized the man in the mirror, Bram thought. Lena and Grandpa had done their best to keep all of the leaflets and pamphlets about him out of the shop – after all, they hated anything to do with highwaymen – but they weren't able to do anything about the posters that were plastered all across town a year or so ago.

The mask hadn't turned her into just another highwayman; it had transformed her into Diamond Jack, the most infamous bandit in all the land.

'Bramble?' Mr Wren said, stepping forward. 'Where's Diamond Jack?'

The police were expecting an answer.

'Er—' She scrambled around for the words. 'Gone. He's gone. That's right. He ran through the shop and out the back and I haven't seen him since.'

'You're absolutely sure?' said the man with straw-coloured hair.

Bram bit her lip and nodded.

Nancy released her. 'Why would Diamond Jack come here?' she said. 'What's so special about Mr Browning's emporium?'

Bram shook away her immediate desire to defend Grandpa's shop, and simply said, 'I don't know.'

'Maybe he needed to buy a gift,' Mr Wren said. 'Mr Browning always stocked a fabulous array of candlesticks.'

Nancy gasped. 'The three people who took your grandpa, it's possible they were looking for Diamond Jack.' Nancy turned to Mr Wren. 'You stay here, watch the girl. Frank and I will check out the back, see if we can pick up his trail.'

'On my own?' Mr Wren said, his voice wobbling.

Neither of the other bobbies replied as they jogged towards the garden.

After a long pause, Bram said, 'If you don't mind, Mr Wren, I'm going to my friend Ernest's house next door.'

The anxiety melted from his face. 'Mind? No, not at all, Bramble. You go right ahead and I'll get back to my rounds.'

Back to the pigeons, more like, she thought with a wry smile.

After the horror of seeing the ransacked shop and hearing the news about Grandpa, Ernest finally calmed down enough to sit at the kitchen table and drink a cup of tea while Bram told him the whole tale from start to finish: the hooking feeling in her stomach right up to the reaction of the passers-by when she ran outside and then . . .

She tailed off. She couldn't *tell* him about the glamour. He'd already looked at her as though she was mad when she'd mentioned the mask sticking to her face, so instead she grabbed the mask from her apron and put it on.

Ernest leapt backwards, tipping his chair and knocking over his cup. 'What?' he shouted. 'Who?' He pointed at her, his words gushing out and smudging together. 'You are not Bramble. You *were* Bramble but now you are not. Now you are . . .' His mouth hung open as his sentence dried up. Sweat beaded on his forehead and his lips paled.

'It's OK, look,' Bram said, removing the mask. She was yet to work out why sometimes the mask was a barnacle and her face a rock, and other times it came away just fine.

'Bramble!' he cried, hauling her into a bone-crushing hug. 'It's you. You're OK.' His entire body was trembling.

'I know.' She patted him on the back. 'That's why the mask was hidden. It's magic.'

Springing backwards, he pointed again. 'You were Diamond Jack.' A huge smile erupted across his face. 'You were *Diamond Jack*.'

She laughed. 'I know.'

'Do it again.'

Bram obliged.

'Wah!' he screamed. The shock had turned to pure glee and he began jumping up and down, his black curls shaking with joy. 'Diamond Jack, you're Diamond Jack. Stand and deliver! My best friend's a highwayman.' Suddenly he stopped bouncing and whispered, 'Say something.'

'Er, what do you want me to say?'

He smacked his hand over his mouth and made a high-pitched squeaking noise through his fingers. 'Great Queen Georgina! You have a man's voice, Bramble. A *man's* voice.'

'Really? I sound the same to me.' She tuned her ear into her own voice. It was exactly as it always was, certainly not that of a man. 'Well, that makes sense if it's just a glamour.'

'A glamour?'

'It's kind of like a trick – the mask tricks you into thinking I'm a highwayman.'

'Eh?'

'I haven't actually transformed into a highwayman, I just look and sound like one.'

He shook his head, confused.

Bram decided the shock and excitement must have shut down his brain. She spoke slowly. 'So someone who's a werewolf actually turns into a wolf. That's *transformative* magic. I'm still Bram, you just *think* I'm a highwayman. It's a *glamour*.'

Ernest's mouth made an 'O' shape and he nodded. 'But I thought magic was dead. It was outlawed hundreds of years ago.'

'That's what we've always been told, but clearly, *this*' – she took the mask off and waved it at him – 'is very much alive.'

Ernest plucked it from her fingers, beaming. 'My turn.'

'Go on,' she said. He cradled the disguise as if it were the most precious thing in the world.

'Thank you,' he mumbled to the mask, before slapping it to his eyes and securing it behind his head.

'Aha!' he shouted, turning his fingers into a gun and pretending to shoot.

But he was just a boy in a mask.

'Well?' he said. 'Am I Diamond Jack?'

She couldn't bear to deliver the bad news, so she settled on a sympathetic head tilt.

His whole body deflated. 'Why not?'

'I don't know. I don't understand any of this.'

'Maybe a mirror will help.'

'Maybe,' she replied, though she couldn't see how. 'There's one in my room.'

He took the stairs two at a time, then spent several minutes watching his reflection try on the mask, all the while moaning with disappointment.

Bram tugged at his shirt sleeve. 'Ernest, there isn't time for this. We need to help Grandpa.'

He let the mask fall by his side. 'You're right. Of course we do.' He took a moment to compose himself, then he took a deep breath. 'So the three figures who took Gramps, they said they were looking for someone?'

She nodded. 'They said "he", they were definitely looking for a man.'

'Diamond Jack?'

'I think so.'

Ernest bit his lip. 'But *you're* Diamond Jack.'

'Only today. Besides, they don't know that.'

'It makes no sense. Why would Gramps have a magical mask hidden in his shed?'

'Maybe he knew the real Diamond Jack?' she replied. 'Maybe the real Diamond Jack asked Gramps to hide it for him when he disappeared a year ago?' But she shook her head. It wasn't possible that her kind gentle grandpa who baked biscuits and sold trinkets had got caught up with an infamous highwayman.

Ernest gasped. 'What if Diamond Jack doesn't exist? What if he *never* existed?'

'What do you mean?'

'What if he's always been a glamour?' He threw his hands over his face and let out a disappointed wail. 'No. My idol can't be an illusion. I refuse to accept it.'

But Bram had gone very quiet and still.

'Bram? Are you OK?' Ernest peered at her. 'You've gone pale.'

She opened her mouth but no sound came out. Her brain whirred faster and faster, making connections and churning up theories. Diamond Jack had disappeared a year or so ago, around the time her parents died. And she'd just found an enchanted mask that was hidden fairly recently, judging from the brickwork in the shed. Perhaps it was hidden a year or so ago . . .

'Bramble?' Ernest said, touching her arm. 'What is it?'

'Did you ever know my papa's name?'

'Mr Browning?'

She lowered her voice, just in case the walls, the carpets, the spiders in their webs could hear. '*Jacob* Browning. Jacob, as in . . . Jack.'

'No way.'

She nodded. 'I think my papa was Diamond Jack.'

CHAPTER

7

'That's amazing,' Ernest screeched. 'You're Diamond Jack's daughter.'

But it didn't feel amazing. It felt like all the air had been sucked from her lungs.

'Ernest, stop,' she said, her voice trembling. 'If I'm right, then this stupid mask is probably the reason Papa's dead, maybe Mama too if she got involved. They were always together, my parents.' She took a great shaky breath. 'The police said they'd died in a riding accident, but they were so good with their horses. What if it was actually a hold-up gone wrong?

Or a duel? What if they were murdered because Papa was Diamond Jack?'

'Oh, Bramble. I'm so sorry, I never thought—'

'And now those thugs have taken my grandpa.' The anger melted into sorrow and she slumped on the end of her bed and began to weep.

Ernest sat beside her. 'We'll find him, Bram. We'll figure out where he is and we'll bring him home. I promise.'

She found some comfort in his words and replied with a weak smile.

After a pause, he said, 'Let's think about it – tell me about the three figures in the shop. What did they look like?'

Dabbing her eyes with the corner of her apron, Bramble cast her mind back. 'Well, I only saw two of them, a man and a woman. The man was huge, with a horrible face that looked like a skull.'

He gasped. 'Mickey Ripheart.'

The name was an arrow to her heart and it was all she could do not to start crying again. That was why he'd looked so familiar. He was one of the most notorious highwaymen around. Anger flared through her body at the fact Mr Wren hadn't bothered to ask her what the kidnappers looked like.

'You know, Mickey isn't like Jack,' Ernest said. 'He's a bad'un. Wicked. He doesn't give anything to the poor. And he hurts people.' He swallowed. '*Kills* people.'

Bram felt sick.

'Sorry,' he muttered. 'I shouldn't have said that. Did you see anyone else?'

'A lady, tall and slim, wearing trousers, and there was a belt across her chest that was covered with knives.'

'Cutthroat Connie.' Ernest wrinkled his face. 'She's got the best knife skills in all the land, well, except for Agnes-the-Blade, that is.'

A wave of terror crashed over her. Someone with the name Cutthroat was not a person she wanted anywhere near her darling grandpa.

'What about the other man?' Ernest asked.

'I couldn't see him.'

'I bet it was Nines. That's Mickey's gang, you see – Cutthroat Connie and Nines.'

'Why's he called Nines?' She almost didn't want to ask, too afraid of the answer.

Ernest held up ten fingers and dropped one from view. 'He lost a finger in a fight.' He paused, seemingly debating whether to disclose the next piece of information. 'With Connie,' he finally said.

'I thought they were friends.' Bram's voice rose with horror.

'They're a gang, they're not friends. Highwaymen that rotten aren't capable of friendship.'

Her eyes welled again as she thought of Grandpa being held captive by this monstrous trio.

'I may be wrong,' he said. 'It may not be Mickey and his gang. There's only one way to be sure.'

A few minutes later, he returned with his scrapbook of highwayman memorabilia. It was brimming with newspaper clippings, wanted posters, and his own sketches and scribblings. Bram had never paid it much attention. Until now.

After a few page turns, her breath caught in her throat. 'There!' she said, pointing at a wanted poster. 'That's the man who took Grandpa.'

The skull face was unmistakable, even drawn in black ink and hiding beneath a dark eye mask.

Written below his image were the words: *Mickey Ripheart. Notorious highwayman and rogue. Ringleader of the infamous Ripper Gang. Wanted for the crimes of theft and murder committed across both town* and country. *Armed and extremely dangerous.*

The letters blurred together and her heartbeat accelerated; the reward for his capture was more money than Bram could imagine, and everyone knew, the higher the reward, the worse the villain.

A sob escaped from her mouth, but she forced herself to keep flipping pages, taking in more wicked faces. Soon, she found the woman with the knives, immediately recognizing the long pale braid and the triangular hat, though her face too was lurking behind an eye mask. The caption below read: *Cutthroat Connie. Wanted in both town and country for theft and murder. Member of the infamous gang known as the Rippers. Considered armed and dangerous.*

The reward was high, though not as high as Mickey's.

'At least we can tell the police who took Grandpa,' she said.

Ernest pressed his lips together as if he was stopping himself from speaking. She had a pretty good idea of what he wanted to say. He said it often enough when he was talking about highwaymen – *the police can never catch them, they're too fast, too clever, too ruthless.*

He was probably right.

Pushing back the tears, she returned to Ernest's book and found Diamond Jack. There were three posters of him in total, each one lovingly decorated with colourful buttons and ribbons.

'I was eight when I did that,' Ernest said with a shrug. Bram didn't believe him.

In the first poster, Diamond Jack was firing his pistol in the air whilst astride a mighty steed. *Papa was always a strong rider*, she thought to herself. The second poster showed him leaning against a tree, checking his pocket watch. The level of detail in this picture was quite amazing, as though he'd happily posed for his portrait to be sketched. Knowing the tales of Jack, this wasn't so unlikely – he'd probably befriended the artist then paid him with a pouch of jewels.

The final poster was an old one, one of Ernest's favourites, a close-up of Diamond Jack's face – eye mask, fine features, floppy dark hair and a light covering of stubble across his jaw. It was like looking in the mirror with the enchanted mask on.

'Papa?' Bram whispered. If only pictures could speak.

Beneath him were the words: *Diamond Jack. Notorious highwayman and rogue. Leader of the*

Brigands. Do not let his charming manner fool you, this gentleman is armed and dangerous.

Armed and dangerous? They just couldn't be talking about Papa. He was as gentle as Grandpa and had enjoyed reading and needlework, gardening and baking. Indeed, the only thing he had in common with highwaymen was he enjoyed horse riding.

Had she known him at all? There was something sharp stuck in her throat, a shard of glass or a piece of jagged rock, that made it hurt to swallow.

'Who are the Brigands?' she asked.

'Goodness me, Bramble. Where have you been? They're a trio of highwaymen – *good* highwaymen.'

'I thought all highwaymen were bad. They steal from people. *Hurt* people.'

'Not the Brigands. Sometimes the newspapers tell lies about them, but they always shoot to miss. And they only ever steal from the rich to help the really poor people living in the villages outside the city walls.'

'But Lena and Grandpa said . . .'

Ernest held her eye for a moment, as if to say, *Think, Bramble. Think.*

'Oh,' she said, the realization sneaking up on her. 'Lena and Grandpa pretended to hate highwaymen so they could keep all of the leaflets and posters out of the shop in case I figured it out.'

'Bingo!'

She paused, turning the information over in her mind. 'But how do you know the Brigands are good?'

'Because people talk, and I've heard of their deeds. Even the folk around here know about the Brigands.' He bowed his head in respect.

'So my dad is part of the Brigands?'

'*Was.* Now it's just Agnes-the-Blade and One-Shot Charlie.'

Papa's friends had been Mr Kipling and Mama, not a knife thrower called Agnes and a gunslinger called Charlie. Sniffing back another round of tears, Bram noticed the reward money was higher than Mickey Ripheart's, which seemed strange considering Jack never harmed anyone.

'If he's good, then why is the reward for his capture so high?' she asked, pointing at the long line of zeros.

Ernest shrugged. 'My guess – he targeted the rich folk, and they're the ones who pay for the posters.'

Instinctively, Bram returned to the image of Jack leaning against a tree; something about it wasn't quite right. She let her eyes travel up and down his form, taking in every detail. Finally, she found it. It was the pocket watch. There was no gold chain dangling from the breast pocket when she was Jack, she was sure of it. Quickly, she put the mask on and, ignoring the strange whooshing feeling, dashed to her reflection.

She was right. No watch.

'So unbelievably cool,' Ernest said.

But she barely heard him. 'Ernest?' Her voice wavered. 'Look here.' She pointed to the pocket watch in the poster and looked closer. It was so detailed she could see the dove engravings. 'This watch belongs to Grandpa. He never takes it off.' She tapped the silver locket her parents gave her. 'When I'm Jack, you can still see my locket. Maybe there are some things that the glamour doesn't work on? Maybe it's the same for the watch. Which means . . .' She tailed off, her throat closing.

'What's Gramps's name again?' Ernest asked.

'Jacob,' she managed to squeak. 'Papa was named after him.'

They gawped at each other for a moment.

When she finally spoke, her voice was pinched yet filled with wonder. 'Papa wasn't Diamond Jack. Grandpa was.'

CHAPTER

8

'Gramps is Diamond Jack,' Ernest said in a low drawn-out whisper. He then jumped to his feet and repeated the words in a shrill blur. '*Gramps is Diamond Jack.*'

But Bram didn't share his excitement. It simply couldn't be true. Her dear grandpa, with his dancing face and white beard, simply couldn't be a notorious highwayman. Yet it made perfect sense – when her parents died a year ago, she and Lena had moved in with him, so he'd hung up his mask to look after his granddaughters. And what about her parents? Did this mean they really had died in a riding accident?

'Are you OK?' Ernest asked.

She nodded. 'We need to tell the police. If they know the Rippers took Grandpa, they'll be able to find him.'

'Won't that get Gramps into trouble?'

'We don't need to mention the mask – they wouldn't believe us anyway.'

He pressed his lips together and narrowed his eyes. 'Really? The police?'

'I know they're rubbish,' she said. 'But we can't very well rescue him alone.'

'We can't, but maybe Diamond Jack can?' He pointed to the mask in her hand.

She shook her head. 'It's a glamour. An illusion. I won't be any stronger or faster, or know how to fire a pistol or throw a knife. And even if I did, it would be three against one.'

'Three against two,' he replied, a little hurt. 'You've got me.'

'I know.' She nudged her arm into his. 'Sorry, Ernest.'

He sighed. 'You're right, I suppose. We'd better tell the police.'

After popping next door to swap his highwayman cape for a multicoloured jacket, Ernest joined Bram on the hunt for Mr Wren. They found him feeding pigeons in the park again, only this time he was sitting with the other police officers from earlier.

Bram hurriedly explained to them that she'd used wanted posters to identify two of the kidnappers. She'd expected them to fire into action and launch a search for the Rippers. But instead, they shared awkward glances and said they were too busy.

'Too busy?' Bram hissed at Ernest as she stomped down the path. 'They're feeding the birds. Why won't they help?'

'I think they're too scared,' Ernest replied, trying to match her pace.

'Because of Mickey?'

'Yes. But also because of the rumours.'

'What rumours?' she asked.

They paused at the park entrance.

'You know how it goes. It's said the Brigands were loyal to Queen Georgina,' Ernest replied. 'And guess who the Rippers are said to be loyal to?'

'The Princess Regent,' she said, recalling the silver

buttons engraved with ravens adorning the Rippers' jackets.

'Yep. Princess Lavinia herself. And you know how much power she's got now – the police are probably afraid to cross her.'

'That's ridiculous,' she said. 'Why are people so afraid to stand up to her? It's not like she's the true queen.'

'Because everyone who stands up to her . . . disappears.' Ernest released his clenched fists in front of his face and said, 'Poof. Into smoke.'

'Princess Beatrice?' Bram whispered, for it was a name that was always said with sadness and regret.

He nodded. 'Poor Princess Beatrice.'

Princess Beatrice was Queen Georgina and Princess Lavinia's youngest sister, who had mysteriously vanished two years ago at the age of thirteen. The Princess Regent claimed she'd relocated to another queendom, but Bram remembered the whispers well. Princess Beatrice was a vocal supporter of Queen Georgina, and had been openly angry at Lavinia's treatment of the poor. Indeed, Beatrice's disappearance was extremely convenient for the Princess Regent. And rumour had it that Beatrice was now dead. Murdered by Lavinia's men.

If a princess could simply vanish, never to be found, then a shopkeeper could too.

Ernest rubbed her back. 'Don't worry. I've got a plan.' He dropped his voice, even though the police were well out of earshot and the squirrels probably weren't listening. 'The Rippers were looking for Diamond Jack, so we offer them an exchange. Diamond Jack for Gramps.'

'Ernest! *I'm* Diamond Jack.'

'Nah, I meant, we give them the mask. It *is* magic.'

She raised her palms. 'But Grandpa clearly didn't want them to find it. Besides, we don't even know if it will work for them. It didn't work for you.'

'Don't rub it in.' He stuck out his bottom lip.

They walked back to the emporium, taking in the bustle of the pedestrians, the clatter of carts and the street vendors selling crisp pastries and roasted eels. Bram inhaled the scent and ignored her stomach as it rumbled.

Ernest scrunched up his face. 'Maybe it's really simple. Maybe we just find their lair, then sneak in and free Gramps. Maybe they leave him unguarded to go thieving.'

'That's . . . not a bad idea,' she said, ignoring the

nagging Lena-voice that kept piping up in her head, telling her to just go home and stay safe.

They began snaking down a narrow alley where washing hung from lines pulled taut between houses.

'OK. So how do we find the lair?'

Ernest grinned, pleased to show off his highwayman knowledge. 'Well, their hideout is probably somewhere in the Crooked Woods, but the Crooked Woods are huge, so we need to narrow the search.'

'How?'

'We start with the taverns. There's one on the outskirts of town where some of the highwaymen like to meet, and we might hear something if we listen out.'

Leaving the alley, Bram snatched a grateful lungful of fresh air. Soon they would be in the nicest part of town, where the palace sat behind iron railings, heavily guarded by men in silver tunics that were once golden. Bram still liked to think Queen Georgina would one day return from hospital, reclaim her throne, and town and country would once again burn with gold.

'Will Mickey Ripheart be at the taverns?' She tried not to shudder at his name, at the memory of his skull face and cruel voice.

'Probably not. He's too busy being a villain to stop for a chat.'

It was a long shot, but it was the only plan they had, so she took a deep breath and said, 'OK. But I'm not wearing the mask.'

'Spoilsport,' Ernest said with a wink.

CHAPTER 9

By the time they reached the tavern on the outskirts of town, the lamplighters had long since been, bathing the cobbles in a flickering glow, and the cold had begun to worm its way beneath Bram's jacket.

'So we're just going to walk in?' Bram said.

Ernest nodded, his black hair shining in the light of the overhead street lamp. 'We'll buy a drink – milk, obviously – and listen in to the different conversations. See if anyone mentions Mickey and his gang. Even better, their lair.'

'Easy,' she whispered. 'Just two kids drinking milk.'

The tavern was nestled in a row of leaning stone houses. Piano music and laughter spilt from the windows, along with an amber glow and the scent of roasted pig. Bram's belly rumbled for the umpteenth time that day; she hadn't eaten anything since breakfast. Hanging above the door was a sign displaying two crossed rifles and the words *The Rusty Bullet* – the sound of it creaking in the wind mixed with the snorting of the horses tethered below.

The sight of the horses transported her mind back to weekends spent learning to ride with Mama and Papa. She'd adored the wind in her hair and the rhythm of the hooves surging through her body, just as she'd adored her parents. But she hadn't ridden, or indeed been near a horse, since they'd died. For a start, Lena wouldn't allow it; she said it was too dangerous, and Bram hadn't pushed, simply because she knew it would make her feel her parents' loss even more. Blinking back the tears, she tucked her locket beneath her clothes and focused on the tavern and the task at hand.

They stood for a moment, just taking it in. Even Ernest, with all his bravery, couldn't seem to make his legs work. It made Bram feel a little better knowing she wasn't the only one who was afraid. She touched her little finger against his – a reassuring gesture.

'For Grandpa,' she whispered, then, pretending she wasn't bristling with anxiety, she walked towards the door, Ernest close behind.

She stepped inside and the noise slammed into her: shouting, braying highwaymen thumping their tankards on wooden tables. Then came the smell, the stench of a hundred unwashed bodies combined with drinks and roasting meat – it coated her tongue with something vinegary and made her want to gag. The Rusty Bullet was rammed with masked men and women and the threat of violence. Magic mask or not, Bram couldn't imagine her sweet grandpa ever coming here.

'They're all wearing masks,' Bram whispered to her friend. 'They're not even trying to hide the fact they're highwaymen. Why don't the police just arrest them all?'

'You really think the police would survive if they came here?' Ernest replied, gesturing to the rabble before them.

One man scratched his chin with a huge sabre, a couple of women were practising their gun-spinning tricks, and a game of darts was being played at the far end of the tavern, not with darts, but with blades, every one of them clustered near the bullseye.

What would Lena say if she could see me here? The thought pushed a rebellious little smile to Bram's lips.

Ernest glanced down at his favourite rainbow-coloured jacket and grimaced. 'I wish I'd worn something a little plainer.'

'You love that jacket,' Bram said affectionately. He'd made it himself – a patchwork of offcuts from his mother's shop – and no other coat could match his luminous smile.

'I know, but I don't exactly blend in,' he said.

'You weren't born to blend in,' she replied.

A rough voice hollered over to them: 'Oi, kids, buy a drink or sling ye hook.'

She spun to see a red-faced barman, wiping a glass with a grimy-looking cloth and staring right at them. He was one of the only people in the whole room without an eye mask or a handkerchief pulled up over his mouth.

Bram ordered her legs to carry her to the bar. 'Milk, please,' she said, as Ernest drummed his fingers anxiously against the drink-soaked wood.

The barman threw back his head and roared with laughter, revealing the pink crinkle of his upper gums where teeth would normally sit. 'You want milk? Go to a farm.'

A maskless barmaid sidled up to them. She had long feathery eyelashes and a crimson dress cinched at the waist with a belt. 'I'll get you some milk, you look thirsty. But then you need to leave, OK? This ain't a good place for kids.'

'Thank you,' Bram and Ernest mumbled together.

Smiling, the barmaid ducked into the kitchen whilst the barman wiped the cloth across his pink moist brow, rubbed it beneath his sweating armpits, and then continued to dry the glass in his hand.

Bram tried to hide her disgust.

'You're a bit young to be out on your own, in't ye?' he said.

'Our parents are nearby,' Ernest lied.

'A bit young to be at the Bullet then?' he said.

'We want to be highwaymen when we grow up,' Bram said. 'It's, er, research.'

The barman coughed and ran a hand through his greasy black hair. 'Well, if it's research yer after, why don't ye try the grub?' He gestured to the pig in the corner, slowly rotating on a metal spit which was powered by a giant wooden turn-wheel.

Bram tried not to gape. Inside the wheel was a small Border terrier, running as fast as its little legs would allow. Grandpa had told her about turnspit dogs, but she'd never actually *seen* one before.

'That poor little thing,' she whispered to Ernest.

'I'll never complain about having to do my chores again,' he replied.

The barmaid returned and popped two tankards of milk beside them.

'Thank you,' they both said.

Bram took a mouthful of milk. It was warm, chunky and tasted of cheese, but she fought back the urge to spit it back out.

'There's pea-porridge if you can't afford the pork,' the barmaid said, gesturing to a monstrous cauldron of something bubbling and sweet-smelling in the corner of the room.

Bram shook her head. 'I'm not hungry. Thank you though.' She *was* hungry, ravenous in fact, but she had no money. Her heart stuttered in her chest; if she had no money, then how was she going to pay for the milk?

'Ernest, have you got any coins on you?' she hissed.

He offered her a wide-eyed head shake.

Perhaps reading her lips, the barman shoved out his greasy hand, palm flattened and waiting. 'Time to pay up.'

Bram desperately patted down her pockets as though some gold might appear.

The barman rolled his eyes. 'I should 'ave guessed. Ruddy kids! Well, you can earn your milk instead. There are dishes to be wiped, tables to be cleared.' He swung his arm at the rotating pig. 'Or you can take over from the turnspit dog, give the poor blighter a rest.'

She was about to object, as she'd only had one sip of milk, but Ernest's grin stopped her.

'We'll clear tables please, sir,' Ernest said.

She only realized why Ernest was so keen when the barman handed them both a dirty cloth and sent them on their way. Of course. It gave them the perfect opportunity to move around the tavern undetected.

Ernest went one way and she went the other, edging around the tables and listening closely to conversations. Bram paused to clean a table beside a couple of highwaymen who were exchanging stories about their last hold-up; no mention of Mickey Ripheart, so she moved on before they became suspicious.

At the next table was a collection of villains trading necklaces and gemstones that clearly didn't belong to them; again, no mention of the Rippers, so she slunk by, cloth gripped firmly in her hand.

She arrived at the next table to find a lady with dark brown skin, black curly hair, and a purple eye mask that matched her long beige jacket. She moved a coin along her knuckles with such speed, such precision, that Bram couldn't help but stare. The coin flashed gold, matching the buttons on her purple coat, all of which bore the symbol of the one true queen, Georgina.

'Aggy, are you even listening?' the man sitting opposite her said.

He had red hair that tumbled into a red beard, and a blue mask that perfectly matched the inky blue of his eyes. His long faded jacket was fastened by a row of golden buttons, each engraved with a dove. Before Bram could figure out what this meant, the lady in the purple mask gave her a smile.

'Ignore Chuck,' Aggy said. 'He's in a bad mood cos the local newspaper said Nines was a better shot than him.'

Bram tried not to look too interested. 'Nines?'

The man called Chuck snorted. 'I know, it's such a stupid name, isn't it? That man couldn't hit a barn with a target painted on it. I, on the other hand, could shoot the smallest, wriggliest gnat from the air.' He shook his head in annoyance, his red beard swaying.

Aggy guffawed. 'Gnats don't wriggle, Chuck.'

'Do you know Nines then?' Bram asked, trying to sound casual.

But Chuck wasn't looking at her any more. He was staring across the tavern, distracted. 'I think that boy's in trouble,' he said.

Bram followed his line of sight and her heart hiccupped in her chest. Ernest was trying to mop a spill from an extremely large man's chest. She could only assume her friend was responsible for the mess, because the man's face was getting redder and redder and his long grey moustache was quivering with rage.

'Oh no,' Bram said, before dashing to her friend's aid.

'This is me clean shirt,' the man bellowed.

It didn't look very clean to Bram, but she thought best not to mention it as she slid beside Ernest and began gushing an apology. Grey-tache wasn't listening. He grabbed Ernest by the scruff of his rainbow coat and lifted him off the floor with one single gnarly hand.

'No, please,' Bram cried, trying to reach her friend, but Grey-tache simply batted her away as if she were a fly.

Bram rallied, then tried again, pulling at the man's arms, but once again, he knocked her away. She watched helplessly as Ernest struggled, his hands scrambling to pull his coat free, his legs whirring helplessly.

'Someone, help,' she cried, looking around the tavern.

But Grey-tache was clearly not to be meddled with, and everyone looked away, everyone except Aggy and Chuck, who stood from their chairs with concerned expressions.

Bram looked back to Ernest. Tears brimmed in his eyes. She had to do something before the man really hurt Ernest. But what could she do? She was just a kid, no match for Grey-tache.

As if trying to draw her attention, the mask grew warm in her apron pocket. Of course. *She* was no match for Grey-tache, but Diamond Jack was. It may only be a glamour, but perhaps his reputation was enough to save her friend. Quickly, heart in throat, she backed towards the bar. All eyes were on Grey-tache and Ernest – even the barman and barmaid didn't notice her – so, ducking behind the table, she fished inside her jacket, hauled out the mask and slapped it to her face.

CHAPTER
10

She felt the familiar whooshing sensation passing through her, then she dug deep into her lungs and found her loudest, meanest voice.

'Put him down,' she boomed.

The piano stopped playing. Mouths opened, glasses dropped, a wave of gasps rippled across the tavern.

Still clutching a wriggling Ernest, Grey-tache tilted his head. 'Well, well, well. If it ain't Diamond Jack.'

'That's me.' Bram puffed out her chest and touched the edge of her coat, hoping it gave the impression she was carrying a pistol. It must have looked convincing, because some of the bravery fell from Grey-tache's expression and he lowered Ernest just enough so his toes touched the floor.

'Now let go of him,' Bram said, trying desperately to stop her voice from trembling.

'With all respect, Diamond, this don't concern you,' Grey-tache said.

She took a deep breath. 'That's my friend you're throttling, and if you don't let him go right now, then—' She faltered. What threat could she use? She had no weapon, no fighting skills.

Another voice piped up, female and strong. 'Then he'll show you just how sharp a Diamond can be.'

It was Aggy. She and Chuck now stood beside her, and they most definitely had weapons. Aggy opened her jacket to reveal a belt much like Cutthroat Connie's, but instead of one, there were two belts, crossing in the middle, adorned with a small axe and even more knives. Chuck began spinning a pistol from each hand, the metal shining beneath the glow of the oil lamps.

Grey-tache immediately released Ernest and his voice became light. 'Well, you little rascal, why didn't you say you were friends with the Brigands?'

'I couldn't say much at all,' Ernest croaked, straightening his jacket.

Bram sighed in relief. Ernest looked shaken, but there was no damage. He stumbled towards her, a smile forming on his face as he took in her new identity.

Grey-tache gave an awkward bow. 'Any friend of the Brigands is a friend of mine.'

The Brigands. Bram blinked. She was standing with Agnes-the-Blade and One-Shot Charlie – Diamond Jack's loyal gang. She'd been so focused on learning Mickey Ripheart's whereabouts, she'd failed to make this connection until now. Her stomach fluttered. The Brigands had known Grandpa as a highwayman, which meant they might know something about why the Rippers were looking for Diamond Jack now. They might even know the whereabouts of the Rippers' lair.

Did they know Diamond Jack was just an illusion? she wondered, though now wasn't the time to ask.

'Nice of you to drop by, Jack,' Agnes hissed through the side of her mouth.

'Thanks,' Bram replied.

'She was being sarcastic,' Charlie muttered.

'Ah,' Bram said, taken aback, but she had bigger

problems right now: a man with missing front teeth was stalking towards her, holding a blade ready to fight.

Bram stiffened.

'Oh, heck,' Ernest whispered.

Toothless squared up to her. 'You ain't no Diamond,' he said. 'You stole me favourite pocket watch in a card game. Don't think I forgot.'

So Grandpa did win it off someone.

She was about to apologize, anything to stop a fight she couldn't win, when the barmaid with the feathery lashes appeared from nowhere and clocked Toothless over the head with an empty tankard.

'You show the Diamond some respect,' she said coolly, as if a huge man hadn't just slumped at her feet. 'He's a hero, and he deserves a hero's welcome.'

'Aye,' the tavern roared.

But a few seemed to disagree and a small tussle broke out towards the back of the tavern.

'Time to go,' Agnes said.

As they edged towards the door, the tussle became a brawl, a terrifying whir of movement and noise. Fists, tankards and even chairs began to fly as battle cries filled the air. The turnspit dog began to howl, then hopped from the wheel and trotted after them as they sneaked through the door into the cool night air.

'Ernest, are you OK?' Bram asked, dashing to her best friend and hugging him.

He let out a joyous whoop. 'Am I OK? Are you kidding? That was amazing!'

Agnes and Charlie were already untethering a couple of horses.

'Thank you,' Bram began to say to them.

But when Agnes turned, all the friendliness had dropped from her face. 'Jack, where have you been?'

'I . . . I . . .'

'How could you leave us?' Tears glistened in her eyes and her face balled up with hurt.

Charlie mounted a grey steed in one easy action. 'There isn't time, Aggy. We need to get out of here.'

Ernest was looking between Agnes and Charlie with an expression of pure wonder. 'You're Agnes-the-Blade. And you're One-Shot Charlie. The best knife-flinger and gunslinger in all the land.'

Ignoring him, Agnes leapt on to a black stallion. 'Jack, have you got your horse?'

Bram shook her head.

'What are you thinking?' she snapped. 'Turning up

after a year, no pistol, no horse. And you've brought a kid with you.'

'I . . . I . . . I'm sorry,' Bram mumbled.

Charlie hauled a grinning Ernest up on to his horse. 'Hold on tight,' he said.

A high-pitched bark rang through the night. Bram looked down to see the turnspit dog by Charlie's horse, brown eyes pleading at Ernest.

'Poor little fella,' Ernest said. 'We can't just leave him here.'

The tavern door swung open, slamming into the wall. The toothless man wasn't giving up on them.

Bram touched her mask, more aware than ever that the magic was just a glamour.

'Quick,' Ernest said. 'The dog, the dog.'

Bram scooped up the terrier and passed him to Ernest, who tucked him beneath an arm.

One-Shot Charlie laughed. 'Excellent. Another member of the Brigands.' Then, with a gentle squeeze of his horse, he cantered down the street in a clatter of hooves, taking Ernest and the dog with him.

'Stop wasting time and get on,' Agnes snapped, pointing to the spot behind her saddle.

Bram paused. Could she really get on a horse after

all this time? Or would the memory of riding with her parents be too painful to bear?

The toothless man rushed on to the street with a crowd of equally angry outlaws. Bram was out of time. So with no grace whatsoever, she launched herself at the horse, slipped, and ended up slung belly-first over his shining, black rump.

'Come back 'ere,' Toothless hollered through his gums.

The crowd ran towards them, all scowls and gritted teeth.

'Hang on,' Agnes said.

The horse lurched, springing into a canter. Bram gripped the saddle with one hand and the stirrup with the other.

'Come back here, you watch-thieving good-for-nothing!' the man shouted after them as they sped away.

'You've got a lot of explaining to do, Jack,' Agnes said.

CHAPTER
11

Soon the pavements turned to soft grasses, and the buildings into trees painted silver by the moon. They'd reached the moor. Even though her arms burnt, Bram continued to cling on. It was strange, being back on a horse. It made her chest ache with loss, but it wasn't as painful as she'd imagined; her heart was still beating and was still very much whole. Had she been wrong to avoid horse riding all this time? She'd always been a strong rider, after all. She pushed the thoughts away; she needed to think about Grandpa, not Mama and Papa.

Ahead, she could make out Rosemary Hill, a swell on the northern horizon, speckled with candlelight from the royal hospital where Queen Georgina was recovering. She glanced to the east – the Crooked Woods came into view, darker than the surrounding night, with trees that clawed towards the sky. She was grateful when Agnes veered the horse towards the Forest of Bells. Now all she needed was to hang on and for her arms not to break.

'Where are we going?' she called to Agnes.

'Don't pretend you don't know.' Her voice was as cold as the night.

At that, Bram fell quiet. She was supposed to be Diamond Jack, and judging from Agnes's response, she'd been on this journey before. If she was going to find out everything she could from them, if she was going to help Grandpa, then she needed to play along properly.

But the rest of the journey, she was distracted by two questions: did Agnes and Charlie know about the mask? Did they know that Diamond Jack was, in fact, her grandpa?

Slowing to a trot, the horses began weaving between tree trunks. The breeze dropped, the scent of sap and moss filled Bram's nose. They'd entered the Forest of Bells, named because of bluebells that blanketed the ground in spring.

The trees stretched into forever and her face soon began to sting from the scratch of low-hanging branches. Could she really pull this off? She already felt close to tears and she was pretty sure Diamond Jack didn't cry.

Eventually, the horses drew to a halt. Bram slithered on to her feet, pretending she wasn't feeling sick and hurting all over, and Ernest, still gripping the terrier to his chest, caught his foot on the horse's tail when dismounting and landed on his bottom with a thud.

Bram tickled the dog behind the ears. His fur was rough to the touch, a mixture of black and tan, and the scent of the tavern wafted from him.

'Bertie,' Ernest said, struggling to his feet. 'That's what I've called him.'

'Hello, Bertie,' she said.

Grandpa loved dogs, so it wouldn't be out of character for Diamond Jack to be making a fuss of him, she decided.

Ernest set him on the ground and Bertie yapped, his whole body moving in time to his wagging tail.

'Where are we?' Ernest asked, looking around.

They stood on the edge of a glade, surrounded by trees and foliage. An oak sprang from the centre, standing proud and creating a collection of hollows within its roots, each overflowing with wild flowers – buttercups, forget-me-nots and cow parsley. And winding its way around the tree was a sleepy, narrow stream, the echo of the moon held in its clear waters.

'Home,' Agnes replied with a sniff.

'Home? But it's a tree,' Ernest replied.

Charlie laughed. 'Look up.'

Bram and Ernest obeyed. Nestled amongst the branches of the oak was a multistoried structure, woven from branches and thatched with reeds. A long rope ladder reached up the trunk and vanished into a cloud of greenery. It looked like somewhere an elf from one of the fairy tales Grandpa told might live.

'Oh my goodness, a treehouse,' Ernest said, his eyes brimming with wonder.

More like a tree mansion, Bram thought, though she was careful to keep her face straight – it was new to her but not to Diamond Jack. She wondered if Grandpa had helped build it. Would she find little pieces of him scattered inside? Candles rolled in flint, biscuit tins, ornaments with notes hidden inside.

'Your friend can wait here,' Charlie told Bram. 'He'll be out of harm's way till we get back.'

'And where are we going?' Bram asked, figuring it was a safe enough question.

Agnes folded her arms. 'There's a job tonight, and we're not going to miss out just because you've decided to finally show up.' She raised a defiant brow. 'Are you coming or not?'

The anger in her voice made Bram shrink, and she had to remind herself that Diamond Jack would always stand tall. 'Er, what's the job?' she asked, stroking Bertie between the ears.

'You'll find out if you come, won't you?' Agnes snapped. 'Just because *you* decided to take a break, doesn't mean *we* get to stop. Things have been getting worse, you know? Much worse.'

Bram didn't know what to say, and the woman terrified her, especially with all those knives stashed beneath her coat.

Agnes shook her head. 'We haven't got time for this. We weren't expecting to have to babysit tonight.' She gestured to Ernest.

'Hey, I'm twelve,' Ernest said in a whiney voice.

Agnes glared at Bram. 'Look. Are you coming or not?'

Bram was scared of the unknown, scared of taking risks, but she needed to fit in with Charlie and Agnes so she could find the Rippers and Grandpa.

'I'm coming,' she said, before she could change her mind.

A ray of excitement shone through Agnes's irritated expression, only to vanish in an instant. 'Well, OK then. I'll get Dusty.' She vanished from view, swallowed by the trees and the dark.

Forgetting herself, Bram began to ask who Dusty was, but Ernest got there first.

'You kept Dusty? Diamond Jack's faithful steed?'

Charlie nodded. 'We always knew you'd come back.' Was it a trick of the light, or were the eyes of the best gunslinger in the land glassy with tears?

Ernest began to clap. 'I can't believe you're going to ride Dusty, Br—' He choked down her name. 'Br–illiant! It's brilliant. Jack and Dusty reunited.'

'Dusty's missed you,' Charlie said.

'So this must be your lair,' Ernest said, pointing at the house. 'Is it? Is it? The notorious Brigands' actual real-life lair?'

'We call it the hideaway,' Charlie replied. 'It sounds friendlier, don't you think? You can go inside if you like.'

'Er, yes please,' Ernest said, before dashing towards the tree and beginning to scoot up the ladder.

Bertie settled at the base of the trunk and yapped at Ernest.

'Hang on, Bertie,' Ernest said, jumping back to the ground and plopping the small dog inside his shirt. 'There, now you can come too.' More steadily this time, he climbed into the boughs of the tree.

Charlie turned to Bram. 'Who's the kid?'

'That's Ernest. He's . . . he's . . .'

Thankfully, Charlie didn't seem that interested in Ernest, and began talking over her in a hushed tone. 'Don't worry about Aggy. She's just really upset, you know, what with you disappearing without a word, but she'll come round. We both are. Upset, I mean.'

Something about him made Bram feel sad, protective even, which was strange considering he was well over six foot, brandishing guns, and had a fine covering of facial hair.

He leant towards her. 'Tell me though, where did you go? Why did you leave? I know you must have had a really good reason. I'll understand, I promise.'

Her mind struggled to keep up with his questions and she had no idea how to explain away Diamond Jack's disappearance, not without revealing that the infamous highwayman used to be her grandpa. Not for the first time, she wished she knew whether or not Charlie and Agnes knew about the magic mask. But she couldn't very well ask them. So she took a deep breath. 'Er . . . it's complicated . . .'

It was Agnes who saved her, reappearing from the treeline with a beautiful palomino horse, almost white beneath the stars. 'We haven't got time for that now.' Her voice was wild. Untamed. 'He can tell us after the job.'

The horse, whom Bram presumed was Dusty, nuzzled her head into Bram's chest as though they were the best of friends. The familiar ache ignited in her heart as she recalled riding with her parents. Instinctively, she checked that her locket was still tucked beneath her shirt. Not only did she want to keep the memory hidden from herself, she also didn't want Agnes and Charlie to notice it and get suspicious.

Gently, she stroked the soft spot between the palomino's ears.

'Hey, boy,' she whispered.

The horse snorted hello, and the gust of warm breath reassured her a little.

'Dusty's a girl,' Agnes said, mounting her own steed with the air of a dancer. 'Wow. You really did just erase us from your lives, didn't you?'

'I'm sorry—' Bram began, but Agnes cut over her.

'We're wasting time. If you want to come, then get on Dusty and be quiet.'

Bram hated being spoken to like she was a naughty child but she didn't want an argument, so she pursed her lips and nodded. Reaching out for the reins, she realized there weren't any. The palomino's coat was a perfect sheet of gold, no tack in sight.

'Where's the saddle and reins?' she said.

Charlie shrugged. He was already saddled up and sitting on his horse. 'You always rode bareback,' he said.

Dread uncurled in Bram's stomach. She was a strong rider, but normally there was something to sit on and hold on to – she'd never ridden bareback before. And she hadn't ridden for a year (hanging on to the rear end behind Agnes didn't count). Could she really manage her first ride since her parents' death without a saddle?

Determination formed in her belly. *For Grandpa*, she thought. Then, gritting her teeth, she grabbed hold of Dusty's mane and lugged herself up, limbs flailing and body rocking.

Ernest's head poked out from above.

'Wait for me,' he called.

But Bram had already squeezed Dusty with her heels and started after the others.

'Please! Wait!' Ernest's voice rose, waking up the birds and sending them clattering through the boughs. 'Let me come too. I was born to be a highwayman.'

'Sorry, kid, not enough horses,' Agnes called back. 'You can't chase down a carriage on foot.'

You can't chase down a carriage on foot. Every one of Bram's muscles tensed, her heart galloping faster than any horse. So that was the job. It seemed so obvious now, they were highwaymen after all, but the worry about Grandpa, the memories of her parents, the constant hunger, and the sheer exhaustion of pretending to be someone she wasn't must have addled her brain.

They were going to hold up a carriage.

CHAPTER
12

Dusty followed the others with steadfast footing, and Bram leant into her neck, partly so she didn't fall off, and partly to avoid the branches that swiped and clawed at her through the dark. Inhaling deeply, she let the nutty scent of Dusty's mane soothe her jittering nerves. She'd forgotten just how much she loved horses.

They paused when they reached the edge of a mud track that carved through the sycamores and oaks. As Agnes and Charlie glanced back at her, she straightened.

'Do you remember the drill?' Charlie asked her.

'Yes,' she lied.

'Of course you do,' Agnes said, pulling her black curls back into a bun and straightening her mask. 'You've done it a hundred times before, haven't you, Jack?'

Really, Grandpa? she thought, though she nodded. 'Hundreds.'

They waited for the carriage without exchanging a word. The forest was filled with the sound of night – owls hooting, small creatures burrowing, the trill of a cricket. Dusty shifted her weight between her hooves.

'Do you think we missed it?' Bram eventually asked, trying not to sound too hopeful. 'The carriage, I mean.'

'Well, it's your fault if we have,' Agnes sniped.

Charlie shook his head. 'We were told eleven. The passengers are coming back from the theatre.'

'Who are they?' Bram asked, even though she didn't want to know – these were real people they were about to terrorize and rob. The guilt was starting to make her feel nauseous. She recalled almost having a heart attack when Ernest burst into the shop dressed in a cape and mask, and that was just his ma's petticoat. *But Ernest said the Brigands never hurt anyone*, she told herself. *And they give the money to the poor.* Yet she couldn't shake the fact that beneath Agnes's jacket was a criss-cross of knives, and tucked in Charlie's belt were a pair of pistols. If they never hurt anyone, if they were so good, then why were they so heavily armed?

'Does it matter who they are?' Agnes said. 'They're rich. That's all we need to know.'

Bram knew that stealing was wrong, she knew threatening people was wrong, but if she objected, if she acted out of character, Agnes and Charlie would grow suspicious and then she would never find Grandpa.

The faint sound of hooves grew in the distance.

Agnes pressed a finger to her lips.

The hooves grew louder, drowning out the thud of Bram's heart. It sounded just like a drum roll. A memory leapt into her brain: the night before her parents died, they'd taken Lena and her to the circus, where the red and white stripes of the Big Top had swelled with the rat-a-tat of drums right before every astonishing act. It wasn't a memory she ever lingered on for long. It simply hurt too much. And there was too much going on to get lost in her own thoughts.

Two white shapes appeared in the distance. It took

a moment for Bram to realize they were horses, thundering towards them and pulling a grand carriage, on which a coachman – wielding a whip and a mouthful of encouragement – perched on his raised seat beside two carriage lamps.

'Yah, yah, giddy up,' came the cry.

Panic wrapped around her chest, squeezing all the air from her lungs, yet when she tried to turn Dusty, she found she couldn't move. Just like in the emporium when the Rippers stole Grandpa, she'd completely frozen.

The sound of hooves filled Bram's head as the carriage was nearly upon them. Opening her eyes, she could now see the coachman's face and the flicker of the carriage lamps as they sent shadows spiralling across the leaves and the path. Any moment now, Agnes and Charlie would burst from the undergrowth and block the path of the carriage horses, causing them to stop.

Yet when the moment came, Agnes and Charlie didn't move, and the carriage blurred past them, the wind stirring her hair and spattering dust in her face.

Had they changed their minds?

'Now,' Agnes roared.

'For Queen Georgina,' Charlie shouted.

They rocketed after the carriage, a whir of hooves and flying mud clarts.

Without permission, Dusty reeled on to the track and sped after them. Bram lurched to the side and fell, hitting the floor with an almighty *oomph* that knocked the air from her lungs.

Catching her breath, she watched as Agnes and Charlie chased the carriage. The path sloped upwards and she realized that they'd been waiting to strike at the base of a hill, when the carriage's horses slowed to climb it.

Bram saw the flash of Charlie's guns as they twirled round in his fingers, the glimmer of Agnes's largest knife as she passed it quickly between her hands.

'Stand and deliver,' Agnes yelled. 'Your money or your life.'

When Ernest had shouted these words back in the emporium, they'd been exciting, if a little annoying, but now they scared Bram.

The horses whinnied, the coachman heaved against the reins, and the carriage ground to a halt.

Bram struggled to her feet, still wheezing. She just couldn't believe Grandpa used to chase down innocent people and wave weapons in their faces. She was close to tears. But still, his kind, dancing face filled her mind. She *had* to find him, even if it meant doing something dangerous, even if it meant doing something Lena would disapprove of. And if Agnes and Charlie realized she'd fallen off, if she missed the hold-up, they'd never tell her anything about the Rippers.

So with quaking limbs, she clambered back on to Dusty, checked her mask, and headed towards the carriage.

CHAPTER 13

Bram watched in disbelief as Agnes heaved open the ornate carriage door to reveal a lady and gentleman dripping in finery, and a little girl, about six or seven, with a pink coat and tight blonde ringlets that reminded Bram of sausages. She felt a moment of relief – surely upon seeing the child, Agnes would close the door and send them on their way. Surely nobody would involve a child in a hold-up?

But instead, Agnes threw a silk pouch on the floor of the carriage. 'We can do this the easy way, or the hard way.'

The click of Charlie cocking his gun pierced Bram's ears as she noticed the black raven adorning the carriage door.

The woman, who was wearing a tall white wig and chalky make-up, sighed in relief. 'Oh, thank goodness.' She turned to the little girl, who was clinging to the folds of her mother's gown. 'It's OK, darling, you can stop creasing my dress. It isn't the Rippers, it's just the Brigands.'

The little girl bobbed up and down in her seat, her ringlets bouncing from her shoulders. 'Does that mean we won't die, Mama?'

'Yes,' the lady said.

Agnes moved, whip-like, throwing a knife so it sliced through the top of the lady's wig, snatching it from her head and pinning it on the wood of the carriage behind with a twang.

Bram slapped a hand over her mouth, muffling a gasp. If the blade had landed just a few inches lower, the lady would be dead.

'Just fill up the pouch,' Agnes said. 'Now!'

'Where are your manners?' the lady said, her voice high-pitched and angry, whilst she clutched her wigless head. 'Not even a *please*.'

The girl released a squeal of delight. 'Look, Mama. Even Agnes-the-Blade thinks you look better without your wig.'

Agnes risked a quick wink in the girl's direction. 'Way better.'

The girl giggled.

Suddenly, a single shot filled the air, sending birds squawking from their branches and Bram's heart jumping around her chest. Terrified at what she might see, she turned towards where the blast came from.

Charlie was holding a smoking gun, pointed at the coachman, and for one awful moment, Bram thought the coachman had been shot. Then she saw an unfamiliar flintlock pistol lying on the ground, its snout mangled by Charlie's own bullet. The coachman must have pulled his gun, and Charlie, being the best aim in the queendom, simply shot it from his hand. There was no blood. No injuries. Just a very disgruntled coachman who rubbed his hand and muttered obscenities.

'Are you OK?' Charlie asked the coachman, concern in his voice.

The coachman grunted.

'Any more guns I should know about?' Charlie said.

The coachman pulled a slimmer pistol from his trouser leg and tossed it to the ground.

Agnes snarled in frustration. 'This is taking too long.' Pulling another knife from her jacket, she aimed it at the gentleman in the carriage, though she didn't let fly. 'Come on, come on.'

The man responded by slapping one hand on his own white wig and grabbing the pouch from the carriage floor, a strange noise escaping his mouth that sounded like a mixture of 'sorry' and 'all right'.

Quickly, he stuffed the pouch with valuables – coins, a pocket watch, a signet ring – then he held it open for his wife.

'OK, Mabel,' he said. 'Don't keep the nice highway-men waiting.'

The lady made a '*humph*' noise, unfastened her diamond necklace and dropped it into the bag. 'I knew I should have worn my rubies,' she grumbled.

Bram felt such overwhelming sympathy for the family. They may have been rich, and the grown-ups may have looked a smidge ridiculous in their white wigs, but that didn't give anyone the right to steal their stuff. In less than a minute, Bram had swung from feeling the need to take part in the robbery, to feeling the need to stop it. But what could she do? Her mask was still just an illusion, and she was fast discovering that One-Shot Charlie and Agnes-the-Blade really did live up to their names.

The lady called Mabel turned to her daughter. 'Let's have your bracelet then, Isabel. If Mama can't keep her favourite jewellery, neither can you.'

When Agnes spoke, all of the hardness dropped from her voice. 'No, it's OK. We've got enough.'

Mabel sniffed loudly and dangled the pouch from the carriage door. 'Well, I hope you're proud of yourselves, you, you . . . scallywags.'

Agnes snatched the bag. 'Actually, we're incredibly proud. This little lot will feed a village for a week.'

She tossed the pouch to Bram, who, upon seeing a bag of metal and precious stones hurtling towards her face, ducked. The bag hit her square on the head and fell to the path with a thunk.

Mabel peeked from the carriage and finally noticed Bram. 'Is that . . . the Diamond himself?' She began fluttering her eyelashes and fanning herself with her hand. 'Well, why didn't you say Jack's back.' She released a shrill titter. 'Henry! Henry, did you hear that, darling? Jack's back. I made a rhyme.'

Isabel stuck her head from the carriage and waved. 'Do your thing, Diamond Jack.' Her ringlets shook – sausages sizzling and popping in a pan – and her face was alight with excitement. 'Do the thing you always do so I can tell all my friends.'

Everyone looked expectantly at Bram, including Agnes and Charlie.

Oh, heck, she thought.

'Jack?' Charlie hissed. 'She's right, it's time to do your thing.'

Quickly, Bram picked through her memories, trying to recall if Ernest had mentioned anything about 'a thing'. He hadn't. If Agnes and Charlie knew about the mask, if they had any suspicions at all that she wasn't the real Diamond Jack, then this would confirm it for sure.

'Go on,' Isabel called. 'Go on, go on.'

Looking at the girl's eager face, she did the only thing she could think of: offered a feeble wave and said, 'Hi there.'

'Hi there?' Agnes mouthed at her with incredulous eyes.

Bram grimaced. 'Er . . . stand and deliver?'

'Enough of this nonsense,' Agnes said, her expression

growing angry. 'Chuck. You can at least remember how to do your thing?'

With a grin, he levelled his gun at the carriage.

Surely he wasn't about to shoot them.

'NO!' Bram cried, alarm pounding at her chest like a fist.

A series of shots rang through the air.

Bram found she couldn't breathe, couldn't speak.

Then the carriage horses pitched forward and galloped away, leaving the carriage behind to rock on its wheels and settle into the mud. Charlie had shot clean through the harness, Bram realized. His aim was that good.

'Long live Queen Georgina,' Agnes said, closing the carriage door and nodding her head.

'How are we supposed to get home now?' the gentleman called Henry wailed.

'You do what the poor folk do,' Agnes said. 'You walk.'

'Bye,' Isabel shouted through the window. 'Bye, Agnes. Bye, Charlie. Bye, Jack.'

Mabel pulled her daughter back, but not before Agnes threw her another wink.

'Bye, Isabel,' Agnes called. 'Stay off the wigs.'

Agnes and Charlie rode back the way they came, beaming at their success, but as they passed Bram, their smiles faded.

'Drop something?' Agnes pointed to the pouch in the mud.

'It's like you've forgotten everything,' Charlie said, shaking his head. 'Even how to catch.'

Exhausted from shock and hunger, and feeling utterly foolish, Bram half slid, half fell from Dusty and grabbed the pouch. Did they know about the mask? Had they figured out she was an imposter? It was impossible to tell, and the uncertainty was making her gut cramp.

With weak, numb legs, she scrambled back on Dusty, adjusted her mask, then followed the highwaymen back down the hill. How she wished she could rip the strip of enchanted fabric clean away and feel the cool air on the skin around her eyes, how she longed to be just Bramble and not a feeble version of someone else.

When Agnes and Charlie rode ahead into the forest, Bram considered riding home. But the impulse faded as quickly as it came, for who would help Grandpa if not her? And she couldn't very well abandon Ernest at the hideaway. No. There was no fleeing this situation, no matter how scary it was.

She broke into the woods, where the soft light of the moon and stars was dampened by a canopy of leaves. There, Agnes and Charlie were waiting for her, their expressions unreadable beneath their masks.

Agnes jumped from her horse. 'Well, that was – illuminating,' she said, stalking towards Bram.

'What do you mean?' Bram kept her voice steady, though nerves jangled through her veins.

'I mean,' Agnes said, leaning against Dusty and lunging towards Bram's face with outstretched hands, 'you're not Jack.'

Bram released a horrified squeal and tried to cover her face.

But it was too late.

Agnes stepped back, dangling the scarlet mask from her fingers.

CHAPTER 14

'How did you get this?' Agnes said.

If Bram had thought her scary before, she was truly terrifying now; her eyes were like two firepits, blazing behind her purple mask, and her hands were clenched into trembling fists.

Even the forest held its breath.

'I . . . I found it,' Bram sputtered.

A knife materialized, blade pressed flat against Bram's chest, handle poised between Agnes's fingers. 'Where?' she growled.

Charlie appeared at the other side of Dusty and

cocked his pistol. 'Answer the question.'

'It was in my grandpa's shed,' Bram garbled. 'Bricked into the wall. We . . . we . . . just found it.'

'You don't just find magic masks,' Agnes said. 'They find you.'

Bram didn't know what to say, so she simply blinked and tried not to cry.

In the tense silence, the hum of the forest sounded so loud.

'What's your name?' Charlie asked, his face softening.

It was all over. She had no choice but to tell them.

'Bramble Browning.'

'Browning?' There was a shift in Agnes's tone, a hint of something happy. 'Did you say Browning?'

Bram nodded.

'We should have known,' Charlie said. 'Just look at the family resemblance.'

Agnes nodded. 'What did you mean, the mask was bricked into the wall?' she said. 'Tell us everything.'

Anxious words spilt from Bram's mouth, so fast, her lips almost couldn't keep up. 'Ernest and I found it behind a wall inside the forbidden shed. Grandpa must have hidden it when Mama and Papa died a year ago.'

Charlie let his gun drop to his thigh.

'Your parents died?' Agnes asked.

Only seconds ago, Bram would have doubted this frightening woman even owned tear ducts, yet now she was clearly about to cry.

'Yes,' Bram replied. 'There was a riding accident.' Every word was a bruise.

'Oh, Chuck, did you hear that?' Agnes said, lowering the knife. 'Her parents died a year ago.' Her voice cracked and the purple fabric of her eye mask was fast turning black from tears.

Charlie's bottom lip quivered. 'So *that's* why Jack left?'

There was a pause, broken up with the odd sniff and sigh, the snort of a tired horse. Bram thought how sad they must feel for Grandpa, losing both his son and daughter-in-law like that.

'Are you OK?' Bram finally asked.

They both nodded. They looked like she felt: tired and sorrowful.

'So when did you realize I wasn't the real Diamond Jack?' she risked asking.

'I suspected right away,' Agnes said as she bundled the red mask into her jacket. 'Your eye colour was wrong.'

'It was?' Bram asked.

'Jack's eyes were always blue,' Agnes said. 'When you were Jack, they were brown.'

Grandpa's blue eyes must have shone through the glamour, just as her brown eyes had. 'So the glamour doesn't work on everything?' Bram said.

Agnes shook her head. 'Certain things shine through the glamour. Things that are important to the wearer of the mask, I guess.'

'So, you knew Grandpa?' Bram said, the story of his disappearance brewing on her tongue.

'We'll discuss it tomorrow,' Agnes said, sharing a glance with Charlie. 'You can stay at the hideaway tonight, then we'll figure out what to do in the morning.'

'But he's in trouble,' she blurted out. 'The Rippers have got him and they're looking for Jack.'

'Tomorrow,' Agnes said. 'We can't help him tonight. Trust me. The morning is better.'

Bram wanted to argue, but she knew there was no disagreeing with Agnes, so she simply nodded.

The next morning, Bram awoke thinking that yesterday had just been a bad dream. But instead of opening her eyes to her neat little bedroom, Lena snoozing in the bed beside her, she awoke alone in the hideaway, a wooden floor bruising her limbs, and the smell of woodsmoke tickling her nose.

She rubbed her eyes. She had slept in the main living area. It was dingy, with a rickety table and chairs, some tatty cushions strewn across the floor, and mismatching crockery and furnishings. But it was also homely. The floor was swept, plants bloomed from colourful pots and warm sunlight filtered through the gaps in the reed roof, washing everything with the colour green.

Standing, Bram stretched each limb. She was stiff, but that was all, and hardly surprising considering she'd slept all night on a hard floor with only a thread-bare blanket and Ernest's nearby snoring for comfort. She figured Charlie and Agnes had separate bed-rooms, or perhaps had slept beneath the stars – that seemed like something highwaymen might do.

Climbing down the ladder, she found Ernest, Charlie and Agnes sitting around a campfire, roaring with laugh-ter while they roasted chunks of meat skewered upon sticks. Bertie was curled on Ernest's lap, enjoying the odd piece of meat that was passed his way. Charlie and Agnes were already wearing their highwayman garb.

'Hi there,' Ernest said when he saw Bram clamber down the ladder. He was repeating her words from the hold-up back to her. Agnes and Charlie must have told him about the whole debacle.

The three roared with laughter. Even Bertie barked.

Bram crossed to them, the dew soaking through her socks and the fresh morning air needling her cheeks. In the morning light, the glade was filled with floating dandelion seeds and the scent of wild garlic.

'OK, OK. So I'm not cut out to be a highwayman.' She began to chuckle too – it was hard not to join in when Ernest was holding his belly and rolling on the floor.

'Not true,' Charlie said kindly. The sun made his beard glow as brightly as the fire. 'When I first started, I was rubbish, and Agnes here couldn't even hold a knife.'

'It's true,' Agnes said. 'I'm lucky my name isn't Seven.' She held up all ten fingers for Bram to see. She was grinning, her face relaxed, and it was almost impossible to imagine she'd hurled a knife at a lady's wig last night.

Bram sat beside them and patted Bertie on his head. 'Are we going to save Grandpa now?'

'After breakfast,' Agnes replied. 'Chuck can't shoot on an empty stomach, can you, Chuck?'

'Can too,' Charlie said, biting down on an apple. 'Just not very well.'

Bram tried to reel in her impatience; she was desperate to find Grandpa, but she needed the help of the Brigands. The help of the people *she'd* been lying to. Guilt swelled in her chest and she sighed.

'Look, I'm really sorry I lied to you,' she said.

Charlie smiled. 'We understand why. You just wanted to help your grandpa.' He handed her a skewer of meat. 'It was really brave of you to go to the Rusty Bullet last night.'

Agnes must have noticed Bram's look of curiosity, because she said, 'Ernest filled in the gaps.'

Ernest grinned, displaying a mouthful of food.

'I hope we didn't scare you too much,' Agnes said. 'It was a bit sneaky of us to drag you along on a hold-up when we knew you weren't really Diamond Jack.'

'And we're sorry we told you Jack rode bareback,' Charlie said.

'He doesn't?' Bram said.

'Of course he doesn't,' Agnes said with a smirk.

Just then, Bram heard the sound of a distant bell echoing through the forest. The chime was picked up by another bell, this time further away, then another, and another, until the whole forest reverberated with song.

'What's that?' Bram asked.

'This is the Forest of Bells,' Agnes replied. 'Originally it was called that because of the bluebells that bloom in spring, but now there's a new meaning. Ever since Queen Georgina fell ill and the Princess Regent took over, every village in the woods rings a morning bell to show their support for the one true queen. The hope is she can hear them from the hospital on Rosemary Hill.'

Bram listened as the chimes eventually faded. The fire crackled and popped, birds sang, and the sun crept over the roof of the forest, casting it gold and pink.

When Charlie spoke, his voice was gentle. 'We've been lying to you too, Bramble Browning.'

Agnes nodded. 'Chuck and I have decided we need to show both of you something.'

'Ooh, I love secrets,' Ernest whispered.

In one swift motion, Agnes and Charlie pulled back their masks.

Bram blinked, and her mouth fell open. Agnes and Charlie were no longer Agnes-the-Blade and One-Shot Charlie, but two kids with grubby faces and worn-out clothes.

CHAPTER
15

Bram dropped her meat skewer and singed her thigh, though she barely felt the pain.

Agnes-the-Blade and One-Shot Charlie were just like Diamond Jack: an illusion.

Ernest scuttled away from the fire, sending Bertie barking and skipping between his paws.

'You're, you're . . . small,' Ernest shouted.

The girl sitting where Agnes had been only moments ago, flashed a wicked smile and waved the purple mask in the air.

'Surprise!'

She had the same black curly hair and dark skin as her masked counterpart, and looked older than Bram, maybe fifteen or so. The knives on her chest jangled as she moved, swamping her slim frame and looking completely out of place against her tattered dungarees and moth-eaten jumper.

'You should see your faces!' The boy who'd replaced One-Shot Charlie turned the blue mask in his stubby, nail-bitten hands. His voice was high and light, that of a boy rather than a man, though he had the same red hair and inky blue eyes as adult Charlie, and more alarmingly, the same pistols holstered in his belt. He looked younger than Bram, maybe ten, and his legs stuck from his shorts like matchsticks.

He's just a child, Bram thought. She swallowed. *A child with guns.* She opened and closed her mouth a few times, chewing on words that wouldn't come out. Only moments ago she'd been looking at two fearsome highwaymen, and now Charlie needed his nose wiping and Agnes had twigs in her jumper.

'Come on,' Agnes said. 'It can't be that much of a shock.' She pulled Bram's scarlet mask from her pocket. 'You must have considered the possibility there was more than one magic mask?'

Bram shook her head, while Ernest said, 'Not once. We didn't consider it once.'

Charlie scrambled to his feet, reminding Bram of a fawn, all gangly legs and big eyes. Standing, he was a whole head shorter than Bram and wore shorts and a woollen jumper with patches at the elbows. His pistols were too big for him.

'There are *three* magic masks, Bramble,' he said. 'I've got one, Aggy's got one, and now you've got one.'

'Agnes-the-Blade cannot be twelve,' Ernest wailed.

'I'm fifteen,' Agnes replied.

'And One-Shot Charlie cannot be a toddler,' Ernest cried.

'Hey, I'm eleven,' he said. 'And I'm still the best shot in the land.' He caught his apple in his mouth then spun the pistols from his fingers.

'Wait.' Bram finally found her voice. 'You actually throw knives and shoot guns? No magic?' Even though the weapons looked real, she still dared to hope the shooting and knife throwing was part of the glamour.

Charlie shrugged. 'It took a while to learn, but I was always good with a slingshot.'

'If you can throw a ball, you can throw a knife,' Agnes said.

Bram jumped to her feet, shaking her head and pacing as she tried to process this new information. 'But you're children, you can't be running around the countryside with deadly weapons. You should be at school. At home.' This was something Lena might say, and Bram hated that she couldn't escape her sister, even in the depths of the forest. But sometimes Lena had a point.

'So we're kids,' Agnes said. 'It just means we've got quicker reflexes.'

'And nobody knows we're kids,' Charlie said. 'Except for you.'

Agnes stroked her largest blade as if it were a pet. 'And there's nothing deadly about weapons if you don't aim them at people.'

'Accidents happen,' Bram said.

'Not for us they don't,' Charlie said.

Bram couldn't make sense of it.

'Three magic masks,' she whispered. '*Three.*'

'Sit down and we'll tell you the whole story,' Agnes said, as she and Charlie settled back around the fire and patted the ground beside them.

Bram sat beside Ernest, and they shared a wide-eyed glance.

'OK,' Agnes said. 'So what we're about to tell you

is top secret.'

'You have to promise not to tell anyone.' Charlie gnawed down to the core of his apple, juice dripping down his beardless chin.

'Promise,' Bram and Ernest both said.

Agnes leant forward so the firelight set her dark skin gleaming. 'Many centuries ago, when wizards and witches lived freely and magic was rife . . .'

'We know this bit,' Ernest said. 'A group of evil warlocks tried to steal the crown, so the Queen banished magic of all kinds.' He circled his hands as if pulling the words from his mouth. 'And because nobody practised magic, it eventually fizzled out . . . blah blah blah . . . get to the good bit.'

Agnes smiled. 'Well, the Queen had magic too, but she vowed never to practise again, as a show of strength to her people. However, she worried about the future queens. How would they manage without the spells that had protected the royal family for years? So her final magical act was to create three enchanted masks, masks that would work for the brave and pure of heart, helping them to protect the Queen and her loyal subjects.'

'She could have made four,' Ernest grumbled.

'Her loyal subjects,' Bram said. 'Is that why you rob

from the rich to give to the poor?'

'Yes,' Charlie said firmly. 'We wouldn't be the Brigands if we let the people starve. It's been hard, hasn't it, Aggy? Especially without Jack.'

Agnes nodded. 'Things got really bad when the Princess Regent took over a few years back. As soon as she was in power, she raised the price of food and rent, doubled taxes, and kept all of the extra money for herself and her friends. People couldn't afford to live any more.'

'And anyone who speaks up against her disappears,' Charlie said.

Bram thought about Princess Beatrice, the Queen's missing youngest sister, and her heart ached with the awfulness of it. Blinking quickly, she tried to be positive. 'But Queen Georgina will get better eventually, won't she?'

'Yes,' Agnes said, her smile stretching across her face. 'Word is, she's recovering nicely. Here's hoping she'll be back and put an end to Lavinia's rule.'

'Is that why the Rippers want Diamond Jack?' Ernest asked, bouncing up and down on his knees.

Agnes nodded. 'Mickey and his gang serve Lavinia.' She spat out the name as if it tasted sour. 'And the

Princess Regent *hates* Jack. She hates the Brigands. She knows that we're loyal to Queen Georgina.'

'Does she know about the masks?' Bram asked.

Charlie and Agnes shook their heads with force, sending their curls swaying.

'Neither do the Rippers,' Agnes said. 'It's a secret that is kept with the Queen and the wearers of the masks. And now you two. No one can ever find out...' Her voice dwindled.

Bram took a moment to smooth out her ruckled thoughts. 'But why kids? Why Grandpa? Why don't the masks choose people who were already strong and tough?'

Agnes slipped her hand under her knives and let it rest on her heart. 'The masks only work for people who are brave and pure of heart, and that doesn't always go with muscles.'

'But *I'm* brave and pure of heart,' Ernest said.

Agnes offered him a sympathetic smile. 'Of course you are. But it's been thought that the masks like to stay in the same family.'

Charlie laid his blue mask on his lap and studied it. 'I found my mask when my dad died three years ago. It was hidden under his mattress. He was called Charlie too.'

Somewhere, a fox wailed, and Bertie snarled in response.

'You were eight?' Bram asked, incredulous.

Charlie nodded.

'What about your ma?' Ernest asked.

'She's never been around,' Charlie replied, matter-of-fact.

'And I found the mask when my . . .' Agnes tailed off. 'Never mind.' Her eyes remained lowered, and Bram knew better than to ask questions; the memory was obviously too hard for Agnes to talk about. Bram knew the feeling well.

'It was two years ago, wasn't it?' Ernest asked, unaware of Agnes's shift in mood.

Agnes nodded.

Ernest grinned. 'Two years ago, Bertha-the-Blade retired and was replaced by Agnes.' He slapped his hands to his cheeks. 'Oh my goodness, was Bertha your mother?'

'I don't want to talk about it,' Agnes snapped, although Bram could tell that beneath her anger lay a deep sadness.

She decided she should change the subject before Agnes drew her knife again. 'It pulled me to it. The mask, I mean. That's how I found it. It was like it was calling to me.'

Agnes and Charlie stiffened.

'It called to you?' Agnes said. 'You never told us that.'

'Is it bad?' Bram asked.

'It means that the mask wanted to be found,' Agnes replied.

'Why?' Bram asked.

'There's only one reason I can think of,' Charlie said. He'd turned so pale his freckles stood out like paint splatters.

He and Agnes exchanged another look, then said in unison, 'Queen Georgina is in danger.'

'What kind of danger?' Ernest asked.

Agnes rubbed her face with frantic movements. 'How are we supposed to know? There's been trouble for a while, but this could mean something big is coming.'

Bram swallowed. Ernest turned his attention to Bertie, and an awkward pause spread throughout the glen.

The wind caught the smoke and sent it spiralling into the trees, and Bram noticed how blue the sky had grown. Mid-morning. Lena would be home by now. Bram dreaded to think how worried she'd be when she arrived at the battered empty emporium. *I didn't even leave her a note*, she thought.

A note! Her mind spun back to Cornelius, the stag's head that used to guard Grandpa's notes about hidden cookies. 'I think Grandpa hid the mask somewhere he knew I'd find it. Maybe he figured out the Queen was in danger when I told him the mask called to me.'

'That's a good point,' Ernest said. 'Why *did* Grandpa hide the mask? Why didn't he just put it on? Then he could have scared the Rippers away.'

'That's the thing,' Agnes said, her features smudging through a thick swirl of smoke. 'Your grandpa hasn't been Diamond Jack for five years now.'

'What?' Bram said, the surprise causing her to squeak. 'But of course Grandpa was Diamond Jack, who else could it have been?'

Suddenly a voice rose from the treeline. 'Me, Bramble. I'm Diamond Jack.'

The voice was so very familiar, yet Bram couldn't bring herself to acknowledge the reality until she'd seen it with her own eyes.

Seated upon a horse and waiting amidst the trees, still wearing a pink gown, her face flushed from a morning's ride, was her sister. Lena.

CHAPTER
16

The shock was an axe, swinging into Bram's chest and knocking all the air from her lungs. Her boring, strict, rule-obeying sister could not be a highwayman – leader of the Brigands, wanted in both town and country, armed and dangerous. It simply wasn't possible.

'You're Diamond Jack?' Bram managed to say. '*You.*'

Lena offered a feeble smile. 'Afraid so.'

Lena looked so strange, sitting astride a piebald horse, leaves in her hair, still wearing her best gown and matching pink bonnet. Yet in spite of the shock,

Bram felt something warm in her stomach at the sight of her sister. The trauma of the past twenty-four hours had left her feeling like she was coming apart at the seams, and Lena was just the familiar thread she needed.

Surprising even herself, Bram bolted towards her, arms thrown wide.

Lena dismounted in one fluid motion, landing nimbly on her satin shoes just in time to receive Bram's hug. They held each other for a moment, just breathing and feeling the safety of family.

Then both girls started shouting at once.

'Do you have any idea how worried I've been?' Lena yelled. 'You didn't even leave a note. I hadn't a clue where you were! I only came here to see if Aggy and Chuck would help. I thought maybe the Rippers had got you too.'

But Bram wasn't listening, she was too busy shouting, 'Why didn't you tell me you were Diamond Jack? The most notorious highwayman in the entire queendom. Here was me thinking you were staying at friends' houses, when really you were holding up carriages. How could you lie to me?'

There was a strained silence while the sisters glared at each other.

When Lena finally spoke, her voice was quick and urgent. 'Have you got my mask?'

'Agnes has it.'

A splinter of fear dislodged from Lena's face. 'Oh, thank goodness. When I saw the shed, I thought the Rippers might have stolen it.'

'No, but they stole Grandpa,' Bram said.

Lena's eye twitched. 'I know. I found this on the counter when I got home.' She fished a note from her chatelaine bag.

Bram had never seen writing look angry before. She read the words, her pulse beating in her ears.

Diamond,

We've got the old man. Turn yourself over or his blood will be on your hands. We'll be in the usual spot tonight. If you tell the police, the old man croaks.

Your old friend,

Mickey Ripheart

The Rippers must have gone back to the emporium at night to leave the note. Just the thought of them sneaking back into her grandpa's beloved shop was enough to make Bram feel sick.

'Oh, Lena,' she whispered. 'What are we going to do?'

The sound of twigs snapping beneath boots caused Bram to turn. Agnes and Charlie stood behind her, scowling, arms folded, and staring at Lena.

Lena's face lit up. 'Aggy! Chuck!' She moved as if to hug them, but Agnes raised her hands.

'You don't get to call me Aggy any more.' Her voice was a snarl, her face set with rage and hurt, her whole body taut as though she could launch into action at any moment.

Charlie began hugging himself, torn between anger and distress. 'I can't believe you just left us.' His bottom lip began to tremble, and Bram thought he might run to Lena and fall weeping into her arms. But instead he said, 'And only Aggy gets to call me Chuck. Get it?'

Lena's eyes glistened, even as she nodded. 'I understand.' She chewed on her lip. 'Did Bramble tell you what happened to our parents?'

'You should have told us yourself,' Agnes said.

Charlie nodded. 'We would have helped.'

'We're your best friends,' Agnes said, before adding

bitterly, 'Sorry, we *were* your best friends.'

Lena wiped her eyes with an angry hand. 'I'd just lost my parents. I wasn't thinking straight.'

Lena suddenly looked a lot younger than her fancy clothes suggested, and a wave of sympathy washed over Bram. It was a dark time when their parents died, a hard time, filled with tears, and a hollow feeling that grew and grew until it felt like they were drowning in it. Hold-ups, danger and adventure just didn't fit into the hollow of loss.

Agnes and Charlie seemed to soften, though they stayed quiet, awaiting an apology that Bram doubted would come – Lena never apologized.

But she surprised everyone by whispering, 'I'm sorry, OK. I'm sorry. It was wrong of me to just disappear like that.'

'Thank you,' Agnes said, before pursing her lips. 'You still don't get to call me Aggy though.' She flounced back to the fire, dragging Charlie with her.

'That could have gone worse,' Lena said. 'Aggy's really stubborn – can't let anything go.'

Bram wanted to say, *It takes one to know one*, but instead she said, 'Where did you get the horse?'

Lena released a nervous giggle and rolled her eyes.

'Oh, you know—'

Bram had a horrible feeling she'd stolen it.

'Where did you get the dog?' Lena asked, pointing to Bertie, who was scampering around the glade, a stick in his mouth.

'It's a long story,' Bram replied, afraid to tell her sister she'd visited the Rusty Bullet.

Ernest jogged up to them, using a skewer as a giant wagging finger. 'I simply refuse to believe it. You're not Jack, you're couldn't-be-meaner-Lena.'

Lena ducked the flying skewer. 'I think you'll find I'm couldn't-be-meaner-*Jaquelena*.'

He slapped a hand to his forehead, nearly poking out his eye. 'Bram! How did we not think of this?'

'We were too busy looking for Grandpa,' she replied.

'All of these years I've been idolizing Diamond Jack, and I was actually idolizing *you*,' he said. 'I stuck ribbons round your latest picture, Lena. *Ribbons!*'

Lena shrugged. 'What can I say? I'm flattered, thank you.' She exhaled, marking the end of their conversation. 'Right, well, I'm glad that's over with. Let's crack on, shall we? Rescue Grandpa.' Hiking up her skirt, she led the piebald to the shelter, calling over her shoulder. 'Skewer me some rabbit, will you, Chuck. Then Bramble here can tell me everything she knows and we can hatch a rescue plan.'

'Don't call me Chuck,' he called back, even though he'd already begun threading meat on to a stick.

Ernest gathered Bertie into his arms. 'What just happened?'

'I have no idea,' Bram replied, her head still thumping.

'And to think how she mocked me,' he said. 'She told me highwaymen were silly. *Silly*, Bram.'

'Oi! Bram, Ernest,' Agnes called to them. 'Stop gossiping. We need to plan a rescue mission, remember?'

Bram grimaced and Ernest smiled at her.

'We've got this,' he said.

Thank goodness for Ernest, she thought.

After they'd gathered around the fire, Lena removed her bonnet and sighed. 'OK, Bramble. It's time to spill.'

'Promise you won't tell me off?'

Lena gave a reluctant head nod, so Bram took a deep breath and relayed the entire tale, starting with the discovery of the magic mask, right through to Agnes and Charlie transforming into kids, though she left out the fact she'd taken part in a hold-up, knowing full well that Lena would tell her off.

Lena eyed her with suspicion. 'And that's the full story, is it?'

Bram nodded, ignoring the guilt of not being entirely honest. 'Yeah, that's the full story.'

Lena scowled and shook her head. 'I can't believe you went into the forbidden shed.'

'That's what you focus on?' Ernest said. 'The one true queen is in danger and Gramps has been kidnapped, I nearly got throttled by a giant moustache, and you're worried about the garden shed?'

'You promised you wouldn't tell her off,' Charlie said as he handed Bram another stick of meat, which she accepted even though her stomach was cartwheeling and there was no way she could eat it. At least it gave her something to do with her hands, something other than throttling her sister.

'I did promise. You're right.' Lena breathed out slowly, as if releasing a lungful of anger. 'So my mask works for you too?' she eventually said. 'Interesting.'

'I thought the magic masks only had one master,' Agnes said.

'So did I,' Lena replied. 'But maybe it's different with sisters. Grandpa was Diamond Jack, then me. We never thought to see if it worked on Bram too.'

'So why wasn't the mask passed down the family line to Papa?' Bram asked.

'It was supposed to be, Grandpa even named him Jacob so he would fit the role. But when Grandpa asked Papa to wear the mask, nothing happened.'

'But Papa was pure of heart,' Bram replied defensively.

Lena smiled for the first time since arriving that morning. 'Of course he was. Papa was good, but he wasn't always brave.'

'I'm not brave either,' Bram said, remembering how she had cowered in the cupboard back at the emporium.

Agnes chuckled. 'You went to the Rusty Bullet, started a brawl, then you rode bareback on a hold-up just to help your grandpa. I'd say that was pretty brave.'

Bram and Ernest started waving their arms and shaking their heads, trying to throw the words back into Agnes's mouth. Even Bertie barked a warning. But it was too late.

'I knew it,' Lena shouted, pointing at her sister. 'I knew you were on a hold-up, you lying toad.'

The hypocrisy enraged her. '*I'm* a lying toad?' Bram replied. 'Your skin is practically green.'

But Lena wasn't listening. 'You're twelve, Bramble

Browning. *Twelve!*'

'Well, you were only eleven when you became Diamond Jack.'

'I didn't have a choice,' Lena said, her voice hardening even further. 'The mask stopped working for Grandpa when I was eleven. It *wanted* me to take over. It called me. It chose me.'

'And the mask chose me too.'

Lena frowned. 'Maybe the mask doesn't know what's good for it.'

'And what's that supposed to mean?'

'A man saw you in the mask, didn't he, Bramble? A man with a little face who looked like a vole.'

'The man with the weasel face,' she replied. 'How did you know about Weasel-face?'

'That's how the Rippers found you. Weasel-face, as you call him, works for Mickey. He's been patrolling our street ever since Diamond Jack was last seen there a year ago, just in case he ever reappeared. If you hadn't worn the mask, then he wouldn't have seen Diamond Jack, and he wouldn't have told Mickey. Grandpa wouldn't be missing right now.'

Tears scorched Bram's eyes and her throat started to ache. The guilt was crushing.

'But I didn't want to try on the mask,' she said, blinking into the flames and wishing she were back in her own kitchen, toasting crumpets over the fire with Grandpa. 'It made my hands move.'

Lena opened her mouth as if to snap, but instead, paused. Her face moved from annoyance to curiosity. 'Really?' she asked.

'Did it do the same to you?' Bram asked.

Lena shrugged. 'Once or twice.' Her expression softened. 'Maybe we should focus on saving Grandpa now.'

Bram nodded, though she kept her eyes fixed on the fire, not quite trusting them to stay dry.

'I can be bait,' Lena said, switching smoothly into business mode. 'Then the Rippers will take me to Grandpa, the Brigands will follow, then rescue us both.'

'And what's stopping the Rippers from just killing you on sight?' Agnes said.

Bram's heart shrank at Agnes's words.

'Oh, please,' Lena said, her voice flippant. 'The Rippers will want the reward money, and they'll get less if I'm dead. Anyway, I haven't forgotten how to fight. I'm still Diamond Jack, speaking of which.' She shoved her hand towards Agnes. 'Mask please, Aggy.'

Agnes glared at her.

Lena rolled her eyes. 'Mask please, *Agnes*.'

Grumbling, Agnes passed her the mask.

Lena studied it for a moment as though reunited with a long-lost friend, then she tied it around her face with tender movements.

'It's good to be back,' she said, touching her fingers to the red fabric around her eyes.

'Er, Lena,' Ernest said.

She bowed and gave a dramatic hand flourish. 'You'll address me as Diamond Jack now, or The Diamond, or simply, Jack.' Raising both fists, she began punching the air as if fighting an invisible man. 'Stand and deliver. Your money or your life.' Her tone was commanding, dramatic.

Bertie threw back his head and howled.

'Lena, seriously,' Agnes said. 'You're embarrassing yourself.'

'Fetch me my pistols,' she told Charlie, still punching. 'We have some villains to hunt and a grandpa to rescue.'

'Lena, stop,' Bram said, trying not to giggle. 'Just stop.'

A look of confusion touched Lena's brow. 'Why?

What's the matter?' Her fists fell to her sides as she surveyed the four faces staring at her. 'Why are you looking at me like that? Chuck, I asked you to fetch my pistols.' She faltered. 'Please?'

Ernest caught Bram's eye and winked. 'Should you tell her or shall I?'

It was Charlie who finally piped up, his voice bright. 'You're not Diamond Jack, you're a girl in a pink dress. And don't call me Chuck.'

CHAPTER

17

For several minutes, Lena sat in a heap, staring at the mask in her lap, and whispering, 'Why don't you work for me?' while the others hovered around her, unsure of what to say.

Eventually, Agnes spoke, palms outstretched like she was trying to soothe a frightened animal. 'Lena, the mask belongs to Bram now.'

'No way. It's my mask. *I'm* Diamond Jack,' she replied, hugging the crimson fabric to her chest.

'I don't think you are any more.' Agnes's voice was so soft, it was almost unrecognizable.

Ernest caught Bram's eye and rubbed his hands together. 'Awesome,' he mouthed.

But it didn't feel awesome. Bram hated seeing her sister so upset, and the overwhelming emotion she'd felt when Lena arrived to reclaim her position as Diamond Jack was relief. Bram didn't want to be an outlaw.

'Anyway,' Lena said, sniffing. 'Bramble can't wear the mask. It's too dangerous. The whole country is looking for Diamond Jack now, not just Mickey and his gang.' She pulled a folded-up sheet of newspaper from her chatelaine bag. 'Look,' she said, waving it as if trying to loosen the words and shake them free. 'The hold-up from last night is front page news, not to mention confirmed sightings at the emporium.'

Bram saw the headline in bold, black letters: JACK'S BACK.

So that's how Lena knew about the hold-up, Bram thought, pushing away the annoyance that Lena had tricked her into lying.

Agnes swiped the parchment, then, gripping it so hard her knuckles stood out like marbles, she began to read aloud.

'*Last night, whilst returning from the theatre, Lord*

and Lady Mortimer-Pimms were held at gunpoint by the infamous band of highwaymen, the Brigands. However, the biggest shock was the appearance of the dastardly villain Diamond Jack, who mysteriously disappeared a year ago. Lady Mortimer-Pimms told us that the Diamond was as sharp as ever, slicing her wig clean in two, and brutally murdering her horses with perfectly aimed bullets to their hearts.' Agnes shook her head in disbelief.

'I fell off Dusty and said "hi there".' Bram couldn't stop the whiney note running through her voice. 'And not a single horse or wig was harmed.'

'Don't believe everything you read in the papers,' Agnes said, tucking the newspaper into her dungarees pocket.

Charlie rubbed his head so his hair frothed up. 'This is bad, Aggy. Really bad.'

'Maybe not,' Agnes replied. 'Mickey will read this, and we want him to think everything's normal.'

'But what are we going to do if Lena can't wear the mask?' Charlie asked. 'We can't ask Bram to wear it and become the bait.' He glanced apologetically at Bram. 'She just isn't used to that sort of thing.'

Bram wanted to sing out across the clearing: *Yes.*

You can use me as bait. I'll do anything to save Grandpa.
But her lungs seized up and all that came out was a feeble cough.

Ernest watched her struggle and spoke up instead. 'Before we went to the tavern,' he said, 'we already had a plan. We were going to find the Rippers, stay hidden, then follow them back to their lair so we could free Grandpa as soon as they left. We just didn't know how to find them.'

Lena signalled her disapproval with a high-pitched grunt.

Agnes, however, tipped her head, a thoughtful expression on her face. 'That'll work. And now we know where they're going to be tonight – their favourite hold-up spot in the Crooked Woods. They'll be expecting to meet Diamond Jack, but we can easily hide. They'll just assume they've been stood up, then we can sneak and follow them back to Grandpa.'

Bram felt a glimmer of hope. This plan was manageable. Hiding and sneaking, especially with Agnes-the-Blade and One-Shot Charlie by her side, wasn't nearly as scary as someone being bait.

'Well all right then,' she said. 'I won't wear the mask, but I'll take it just in case.'

Lena jumped to her feet in a swirl of pink silk. 'Bramble Browning, there is absolutely no way I am letting you sneak into the Rippers' lair. Do you hear me?'

Bertie, who'd previously been snuffling around the undergrowth, ran to Lena and started to growl.

'What?' Bram replied, taken aback. 'But I want to help.'

'Can you shoot? Can you throw a knife? Can you even throw a punch?' Lena mimed each action along to the words and Bertie scampered behind Ernest, his fur trembling.

'Of course not,' Bram said. 'I'm twelve and I work in a shop.'

'My point exactly,' Lena said.

'But we won't be fighting,' Bram said. 'We'll be sneaking.' In desperation, she turned to Agnes and Charlie. 'Tell her I can come. There's four horses and I want to help.'

'I don't know.' Agnes lowered her eyes. 'It's why we waited until this morning to hatch a rescue plan. You see, you told us yesterday that Lena was away overnight, and we had a hunch that she'd come here after realizing you were missing. She would need our help to find you.'

'And *we* needed her help to rescue Grandpa,' Charlie added.

'It's going to be dangerous,' Agnes said. 'And you're not really—' Her words faded.

'You're not cut out to be a highwayman,' Lena finished for her. 'You don't know how to use any weapons and you're just not hero material.'

'Ouch,' Ernest said.

Fury exploded through Bram's body. She jumped to her feet, heart thumping, limbs trembling. Ever since her parents had died, Lena had been like a jailer, lecturing her about risk and danger, wrapping her in suffocating cotton wool, and Bram had gone along with it, knowing that her big sister was hurting and just wanted to keep everyone safe. Yet all the while, Lena had been Diamond Jack.

Bram stamped her foot. 'Maybe I'd be more gutsy if you hadn't treated me like a little kid for the past year.'

'You *are* a little kid,' Lena shot back as she rose to her feet, clutching the mask. 'You're not coming and that's the end of it.' Suddenly she let out an ear-splitting screech. 'Ow!' She dropped the mask and shook her hand as though stung by a wasp. 'It burnt me,' she said, gesturing to the mask. 'It was hot as a poker.'

A scurry of paws and Bertie swooped in, grabbing the mask in his teeth and carrying it to Ernest, his tail wagging all the way.

'Good boy,' Ernest said, bending down to tickle the dog behind his ears. 'Good, Bertie-boos.' He eased the mask from the terrier's muzzle, then held it for a moment. 'Feels cool to me.'

'See,' Bram said, her voice smug. 'The mask wants me.'

Lena stormed towards him. 'Ernest, give me the mask.'

'No way,' he said, balling it up and lobbing it over her head towards Bram. 'And it isn't your mask any more, it's Bram's.'

Bram caught it with tingling fingers and wrapped it around her head. She felt the whoosh, the fizzing in her veins, then Lena, who was rushing towards her, fingers outstretched like talons, froze on the spot, her determined expression draining away to leave behind a look of disbelief; her fingers relaxed and fluttered to her sides.

'Oh, Bramble,' she said, looking her up and down. 'You're Jack. You're really Jack.'

'I did tell you,' Bram replied.

'I know, I know, and I believed you, but to actually see it.' She turned to Agnes and Charlie. 'Seriously! Was my voice ever that deep?'

They nodded.

'If things go wrong,' Bram said, 'if the Rippers return early to the lair, I can put the mask on and distract them. I can lead them away on Dusty. They'll be far too busy trying to catch me to worry about Grandpa.'

'But will you be able to ride that fast?' Lena said, then she added in a quiet voice, 'Are you ready for that?'

'I have to try,' Bram said. Her locket seemed to grow heavier round her neck, colder against her skin. She adjusted the chain, trying desperately not to think about her parents.

Lena pressed her lips together, deep in thought. 'If they get too close, you can take off the mask, then you're just a girl lost in the woods. They don't know about the mask, so they'll have to believe you.'

'Good thinking,' Bram said.

Lena didn't speak for a moment as several different emotions crossed her face. 'OK. OK,' she said finally. 'I'm not happy about it, but it's the best plan we've got.'

CHAPTER

18

The rest of the morning was spent preparing for the rescue mission; Agnes sharpened her blades, Charlie cleaned his guns, and the others covered hats and jumpers with moss, leaves and twigs so they would blend into the forest that night. Lena found an old sewing kit stashed in the hideaway, one she'd used to darn the Brigands' clothes before she'd left them. She gave it to Ernest so he could fix coiled ribbons of ivy around the sleeves. His stitches were the neatest Bram had ever seen.

At midday, Lena and Agnes took Bram further into

the woods, where the stream joined a much wider vein of water.

'We thought you might be sick of rabbit,' Lena said, hiking up her skirt and kneeling at the water's edge.

Bram peered at the silver dashes of fish that whipped between the pebbles. 'Have you got a fishing rod?'

'She doesn't need a rod,' Agnes said, voice flat.

'I most certainly do not.' Lena's hands hovered just over the surface of the water as she tracked a plump fish meandering across the riverbed. Suddenly, in a whir of movement, she sliced her hand through the water and yanked the creature into the air.

It was an impressive sight, and Bram was pretty sure this was less about finding lunch and more about showing off and making Bram feel small. It worked. Bram swallowed – not only could she not throw a knife or aim a gun, she couldn't catch a fish with her bare hands. She couldn't help but think she'd never really known her sister at all.

The creature flipped and twisted in Lena's fingers, its mouth helplessly gulping at the air, and Bram felt a sudden wave of sympathy washing over her. She knew exactly how it felt to suffocate in Lena's grip, after all.

'Put it back,' she cried, shoving Lena's arm.

The fish slipped free and with a victorious splash, landed in the stream and shot away.

'Hey!' Lena said. 'What did you do that for?'

'I . . . I . . . I'm sorry. It just looked so sad.'

'Fish don't look sad.' Her cheeks grew red. 'How utterly ridiculous.'

'Hey,' Agnes said. 'Go easy on her.'

'And how will going easy help?' Lena snapped. 'How is she going to be Diamond Jack if she can't even cope with a sad-looking fish?'

Lena had an annoying habit of saying Bram's deepest insecurities out loud.

'Well, maybe I don't want to be a highwayman because stealing is wrong,' Bram said, her neck growing hot, her chest tightening. 'Scaring people is wrong. You pretend to be all perfect when really you're just a . . . a . . . thief.'

Lena looked as if she'd been slapped. 'Is that really what you think?'

'Yes,' she said, meeting her sister's gaze with a rigid, angry face.

'Fine.' A mixture of hurt and anger crossed Lena's face, then she turned and stomped back to the glade, leaving Bram and Agnes staring awkwardly at the river.

'It looks like we're having rabbit again,' Bram eventually said.

'She's just looking out for you,' Agnes said. 'It's what sisters do.'

Bram slumped beside the river's edge. 'So why is she so awful to me?'

Agnes sat beside her and dangled her feet in the water. 'There's so much going on right now, she's worrying about everything so it all comes out in the wrong way. Look, I've got siblings too, and Lena has her moments but she's really not bad.'

'She's not?'

'Lena's mean because she wants to protect you. My sister was mean because . . .' Agnes seemed to search the water for the right words. 'Well, because she was mean through and through and wanted to hurt me. She was always envious . . . she thought I was . . . It doesn't matter.'

Bram studied Agnes's face. 'Is that why you didn't want to talk about your family earlier?'

She sniffed. 'Yeah.' Her eyes welled with tears that she quickly blinked away. 'When this is all over, you can go back to normal. Just don't be too hard on her, that's all I'm saying.'

'OK,' Bram said, though she wasn't sure she meant it.

CHAPTER

19

Lena avoided Bram all through lunch, then she disappeared inside the hideaway without a word. Bram was just beginning to worry, when her sister came down the ladder, with a wicker basket hanging from her arm.

'Bramble, Ernest, I need to show you something,' she said.

'What is it?' Bram said as she laid out more strips of ivy for Ernest. The wicker basket was overflowing with velvet pouches and her interest grew.

'You'll see. Follow me,' Lena said, stepping into the

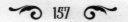

dappled shadows of the forest.

She still wore her pink dress, though soil crept up the hemline and dead leaves clung to the bodice. Bram fancied that she looked like a girl from a fairy tale, about to take a basket of freshly picked strawberries to her grandmother. An image of a wolf – long ears and even longer teeth – swam into her mind. His face was skull-like and she shuddered.

Agnes was right, Lena wasn't so bad really.

They left Charlie and Agnes in charge of the camouflage, and trudged through the trees in silence, except for Bertie, who happily yapped the whole while; birds scattered from nearby branches and butterflies danced from blooms. Sunshine broke through the leaves, mottling their skin and the mulch beneath their boots with bright yellow light.

'Stand and deliver,' Ernest yelled, as he jumped out from behind trees, his multicoloured jacket vivid amongst the green.

'Does he ever stop?' Lena muttered.

'Never,' Bram replied.

'And what's with the coat?' Lena said.

'Hey,' Ernest said. 'I like this coat. I made it myself.' He glanced at her dress and grinned a wicked grin.

'You know that's imitation silk, right? You can tell because it doesn't shimmer in the sun quite as much as real silk.'

Lena glared in response.

Bram's feet began to ache just as they reached a large clearing, filled with a huddle of stone cottages and the sound of children laughing.

Lena gestured to them to stop at the treeline. 'Bramble, put on your mask.'

'I am not going to rob a village,' she said, horrified.

Her sister simply laughed. 'Oh, please, we're going to *give* to the village.' She lifted the wicker basket. 'These pouches are filled with coins, money from hold-ups. I know I always told you that stealing is wrong, and it is, of course it is, but starvation is worse.'

Relieved, Bram pulled the mask from her apron pocket and tied it to her face.

Whoosh. Fizz.

'That will never stop being cool,' Ernest said, scooping up a wriggling Bertie.

On entering the village, Bram realized just how poor it was; the cottages looked like they were falling in slow motion, roofs slipping into walls and walls crumbling into mud. The people milling about looked tired and slow. Bram lived in the well-to-do part of town surrounded by busy merchants and people ready to buy. Her family weren't rich, but they always had enough to eat, fresh clothes, and a roof that kept out the rain. Bram went to school and had gone riding every weekend before her parents died. She'd never seen anything like this, and she took a moment to just take it all in.

A couple of women with ragged clothes were tending to a herd of livestock inside a ramshackle pen. Pigs, sheep and a flea-bitten cow. A shirtless man washed clothes in a bucket of steaming soapless water, his ribs poking from his skin like rods, while a girl pegged dripping shirts on a wonky line. Barefoot children ran between the houses, laughing and trying to catch each other, while a group of bone-thin adults knelt over a vegetable patch, easing up weeds and emptying chipped clay pots of river water on to the crops.

Lena cleared her throat and the shirtless man spotted them.

'Jack's back,' he shouted, punching a fist into the air.

The children ran towards Bram, whooping and clapping.

'Hooray for Jack,' they called. 'Hooray for the Diamond.'

Bram knelt and greeted each one with a smile and a hello. Tiny hands touched Bram's mask and pulled at her clothes, and she laughed at the sheer joy on their grubby faces.

'Oh, Jack!' A lady with long blonde hair strode towards them. 'Where have you been?' She wore a frayed dress and clutched a baby to her hip. 'We've been so worried about you.'

Bram glanced at her sister, who mouthed, 'Betty.'

'Betty,' Bram said, standing and smiling broadly. 'It's lovely to see you again. I'm sorry I haven't been able to visit for a while.'

Betty beamed; her skin was so pale beneath the midday sun it was almost transparent. 'That's OK. Agnes and Charlie have been instead. But we've missed you.'

'I'm here now,' Bram replied, tickling the baby under the chin, who chuckled in response. Her heart ached at the sight of his tattered clothing.

The other grown-ups arrived and crowded around her, shaking her hand, while Lena hissed their names into her ear. *Fred. Sally. Paul . . .*

Lena stepped forward, basket raised. 'Jack's brought you a pouch of coins, one for each family.'

Betty's face crumpled. 'Oh, Jack. A whole pouch each?' Her eyes grew watery and she turned towards her baby, pretending to steal a kiss, though Bram knew she was really hiding her tears. 'We can get Jack Jack here a cot.'

'Jack Jack?' Bram said.

'We named him after you. He's the third Jack in the village now.'

'I'm Jackie,' said a young girl with a muddy T-shirt and brightly coloured flowers threaded through her dark braid. She was holding a toy gun, made from two sticks bound together by string, which she pointed playfully at Ernest. 'Stand and deliver,' she shouted.

With all his usual gusto, Ernest pretended to be shot, and the girl erupted into giggles.

'And I'm Jacoby,' said a boy with a stick-sword in his hand. 'Your money or your life.'

'Wow,' Bram said. 'That's—' She spluttered on her words. These people were so grateful to Diamond Jack they'd named their children after him. And it was in that moment Bram realized that her sister hadn't been running around the forest having fun and playing at being a highwayman, she'd been putting her life in danger to feed and help families. 'That's just lovely,' she managed to say. Then she began handing out the velvet pouches, each of which was received with a mixture of smiles and tears.

Whilst saying goodbye, Bram noticed an empty, upturned wooden crate with a wreath of wild flowers propped against it and a golden, dog-eared royal flag folded on top.

'What's that?' she asked.

Betty smiled. 'In memory of Princess Beatrice, the missing princess.' Her smile flipped into a scowl. 'That awful Princess Lavinia! As if it isn't bad enough she wants us all to starve, she had to make Princess Beatrice disappear too? How could anyone hate their own sister so much?'

Bram thought of the Princess Regent, of how she'd made her youngest sister, Beatrice, disappear, and how she was still trying to keep hold of the throne from Queen Georgina. Her heart welled with guilt. Lena may have been bossy and self-righteous, but Agnes was right – all Lena had ever done was try to protect her.

She met Lena's eye and gave her a sheepish smile. 'At least most sisters are good.'

Lena returned her smile.

Just then, Bram felt a tugging on her sleeve, and

looked down to see a young child with a shock of white hair grinning up at her.

'Jack, Jack, do your thing,' the child said, excitement radiating from her face.

Panicked, Bram glanced at Lena, who replied with a helpless grimace. Bram still had no idea what 'the thing' was, and she couldn't very well ask her sister in front of everyone.

'Oh, er, we need to go to the next village,' she said. 'Maybe next time.'

'Pleeeease,' the child said.

Other children began joining in until there was a mass of begging faces and pressed together palms, a chorus of pleads.

Lena whispered hurriedly in her ear:

> '*Thanks for the pleasure,*
> *Of stealing your treasure,*
> *And remember to tell your friends,*
> *That Diamonds may shine,*
> *And look mighty fine,*
> *But they always cut deep in the end.*'

Bram blinked, trying to take in the ditty over the

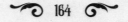

pleads of the children, the excited faces of the villages, and the grunts and squeaks of the animals.

'Just say it,' Lena hissed. 'With pzazz.'

'Er, OK then,' she said, rolling up her sleeves.

The village fell quiet in anticipation, even Bertie stopped yapping, so Bram put on her best highwayman stance – feet parted, hands on hips, chest puffed out – and lifted her voice so it sailed over the treetops. 'Thanks for the pleasure, of eating your treasure.'

The children started to laugh.

'You don't eat treasure,' the white-haired child said with a giggle.

Bram laughed nervously and tried desperately to recall Lena's words. 'Er, remember your friends are shiny,' she said, her posture sagging as all the confidence left her.

But when she looked at the children, they were smiling and laughing as if it was the best thing they'd ever heard.

'Go on,' came the chant. 'Go on, Jack. Go on.'

Betty slapped him on the back. 'Oh, Jack, that's hilarious. Do keep going, a good guffaw is what we all need.'

Bram felt a spark in her chest, and when she smiled,

it was broad and genuine. They didn't care if she got it wrong, they were just so happy to see her and to be able to pay their rent.

Straightening her back, she raised a hand as if about to perform an opera.

'Thanks for the pleasure of eating your treasure, and remember your friends are shiny. Finish your greens, and don't be mean.' She cast around for a word rhyming with shiny, and eventually shouted, 'Cos in the end, we're all slimy.'

Ernest began cheering from the pen, the villagers laughed, and the children jumped up and down, clapping and shouting: 'That was great.' 'Even better than usual.' 'Mummy, Daddy, can I have that as my lullaby now?'

Lena sighed. 'That was ridiculous, but you kind of pulled it off. Now come on. We need to get Grandpa.'

CHAPTER
20

Back at the hideaway, Bram mounted Dusty, her hands shaking and her stomach rolling with anxiety. *At least I've got a saddle and reins this time*, she thought.

'You be careful,' Ernest said, adjusting her stirrups so they were the perfect length for her legs.

'I will,' she said, patting her apron pocket. 'I've got the mask, just in case.'

He lowered his eyes. 'I wish I could come too.'

'I know, but there aren't enough horses. Besides, someone needs to look after Bertie.'

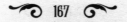

The terrier yapped from between Ernest's feet, and as Ernest bent to ruffle his fur, Bram noticed that he was no longer wearing his favourite coat.

'Hey, where's your jacket gone?' she asked.

'I left it in the hideaway.'

'But you never take it off.'

Ernest replied with a shrug.

'Is it cos of what Lena said back in the forest?' she asked.

'Nah. Like I'd take fashion tips from her.' He winked. 'I just have this feeling my coat is destined for greater things.'

She was about to ask him what he meant, when Lena approached them, mounted on her piebald horse. She'd swapped her dress for some of Agnes's clothes – a woolly jumper and a pair of patched trousers – and a thick strap of leather that hung from her hips. It was completed with a pair of holstered pistols and sheathed knives.

'Are you ready?' she asked, looking a little nervous as she adjusted her position on her horse.

'Doesn't Bram need a weapon?' Ernest said, admiring Lena's makeshift belt. 'She may need to protect herself.'

Lena shook her head. 'She could accidentally hurt someone, or worse still, hurt herself. Guns aren't toys.'

'Knives?' he asked.

'Knives aren't toys either.'

He tipped his head. 'What about one knife?'

'Absolutely not.'

'Well, you can have my new pistol,' Ernest said, handing Bram a toy gun made of sticks. 'A little girl at the village gave it to me. You can at least bop someone over the head with it if you need to.'

'Thanks, Ernest,' Bram replied, tucking it into the band of her apron and feeling grateful for her best friend.

'Oh, and this, some leftovers in case you get hungry.' He produced one of the velvet money pouches. The material was soggy and smelt like Mr Kipling's butcher's shop. It clearly wasn't filled with money any more. She dropped it in her apron pocket and thanked him.

'Let's do this,' Agnes said, steering her horse past Bram. She wasn't wearing her mask yet, and it still shocked Bram to see her slender frame swamped by two blade belts.

Charlie followed Agnes on his grey mare, his little legs barely reaching the stirrups. 'Bye, Ernest,' he called.

'Bye, notorious highwayman who is so very small,' Ernest called back.

The pair were swallowed by the treeline.

Lena trotted after them. 'Come on, Bramble.'

'Look after her,' Ernest called.

'What do you think I've been doing for the past year?' Lena replied.

Bram gave him one last sympathetic smile. 'I'll be careful, I promise.'

'And?'

'And I promise I'll tell you every single detail when I get back.'

'OK,' he said, squeezing her hand. 'Then you may go.'

They both laughed, though it sounded fragile and faded quickly, then she turned Dusty and headed into the closing shadows of the Forest of Bells.

CHAPTER
21

Entering the Crooked Woods was like diving into murky water; the usual sounds of the forest were gone. Birds were too scared to chitter, animals were too afraid to forage, and the late evening sun struggled to pierce through the dense branches. The stench of rotting vegetation hung between the twisted trees like mist and Bram found herself hankering after the fresh, sunlit green of the Forest of Bells.

'This place is grim,' she said. The grey bark of the surrounding trunks muffled her voice.

'Just stay close,' Lena replied.

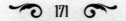

Somewhere, a dog howled and Dusty released an uneasy whinny.

'It's OK, girl,' Bram whispered into her soft ears.

They wove between the endless trunks, ducking beneath thick cobwebs while leafless branches clawed at their faces. Bram shuddered. *Well, of course the Rippers' territory is something straight out of a ghost story*, she thought. After a while, they picked up a dirt path that cut through the colourless trees. Bram had never been so relieved to see the sky. The dusk sank around them and she could just see the outlines of the stars.

'Where are we going?' she asked.

Charlie glanced over his shoulder, his face glowing like a miniature full moon. 'There's a tree tunnel coming up – it's the Rippers' favourite spot. Connie climbs the tallest tree, then when Mickey and Nines are holding up a carriage, she drops on to the roof and gives the passengers the fright of their life.'

Agnes tutted, loud enough to be heard above the thunk of her horse's hooves. 'Sometimes she jumps in front of the horses so they panic and tip the carriage.'

'That's awful,' Bram said, imagining how scared little Isabel would have been had her carriage fallen on its side when they held it up.

'That's the Rippers for you,' Lena said. 'They prefer to drag out the fear.'

Bram swallowed.

'We better hide the horses soon,' Agnes said. 'The tunnel isn't far now.'

Bram was reluctant to leave Dusty. She'd forgotten just how soothing horses were, with their soft earthy scent and the steady plod of their hooves. Riding Dusty had made her feel closer to her parents than she had all year. That said, she didn't want Dusty anywhere near Mickey and his gang, so she tethered her faithful steed far from the path with the other horses, fed her an apple, poured her a dish of water, then looped her arms round her muscular neck.

'We shouldn't be too long,' she whispered.

Dusty flared her nostrils in reply.

'They'll be fine,' Lena said as Bram headed back up the path. 'They'll probably be grateful for the rest.'

Agnes and Charlie walked ahead, carrying the duffel bags stuffed with camouflage gear, and soon enough, the trees lining the path began reaching towards the opposite side with greedy fingers, closing off the night sky.

'The tree tunnel,' Agnes said.

'Now what?' Bram asked, noticing a drop in light and temperature as they stepped through. Hugging herself, she shivered. A vision of her bed appeared in her mind's eye. Warm, soft, safe. How she missed her lovely bed.

'Now we hide,' Lena said. 'The Rippers work at night, so we've got a bit of a wait. At least there's time to get our camouflage gear on.'

Just then, the distant rumble of an approaching carriage travelled through the soles of Bram's shoes.

'Mickey?' she asked, ashamed of the fear twisting through her.

'No. The sun hasn't set,' Agnes said, touching her leather criss-cross of knives.

Charlie reached towards his gun holster. 'And Mickey doesn't travel by carriage. A chance for a quick hold-up, I think.'

'Get off the path,' Lena said, pointing at the wall of trees. 'Now.'

But Agnes and Charlie were grinning, their hands already diving into their pockets for their masks.

'Don't even think about it.' Lena's voice was a warning.

They pulled their masks on. The two raggedy

children were instantly replaced by a pair of intimidating highwaymen wrapped in terrifying weapons. It still surprised Bram to see their tall, athletic forms, their grown-up faces, equipped with cheekbones and – in Charlie's case – facial hair.

'Aggy, Chuck,' Lena snapped. 'You aren't seriously considering holding up a carriage *now*?'

'Seems a shame to waste it,' Agnes said with a wink. 'And I'll thank you for referring to me as Agnes-the-Blade.'

Charlie drew his pistol with hands the size of spades. 'And One-Shot Charlie.' His voice was now so deep it almost made Bram giggle.

Lena released a huff of annoyance. 'Unacceptable. Simply unacceptable.'

The mask inside Bram's apron began warming her stomach just like back in the tavern. '*Remember me?*' it seemed to say.

Instinctively, her fingers reached for it.

'Don't you dare,' Lena said.

Bram allowed herself to touch the fabric, wishing she were brave enough to rebel against Lena.

It stuck to her fingers.

'No, no, no,' she muttered, shaking her hand; she'd

completely forgotten about the mask's ability to adhere.

'Bramble Browning.' Lena waved an angry hand at her. 'Put that mask down right now.'

'I'm trying,' she said, even as her hands lifted to her face.

'Bramble!' Lena's voice was a squawk.

'It isn't me.' Her brain ordered her hands to stop, but the mask was in control, and before she knew it, her fingers were fixing the scarlet fabric behind her head. The whooshing spread through her body, her blood fizzed.

Agnes and Charlie shared a look.

'If Diamond Jack is here, we may as well use him,' Agnes said.

Bram hated to admit it, but a small part of her was pleased the mask had insisted on being worn, because deep down, there was something about being Diamond Jack that made her feel good. It chose her, not Lena. Whilst staying in the shop all year had made her feel safe, it had also left her feeling cramped and confined. Wearing the mask was like stretching out her limbs after a long sleep.

The carriage was now visible. A drum roll of

hooves. Once again, the circus flashed into her mind. She longed to linger on the memory, on her parents' laughing faces as the human cannonball shot through the air, on their cheers as the women in leotards soared between trapezes. But she was scared of the pain of missing them. Besides, now really wasn't the time.

Lena stomped towards her. 'Take that mask off right now. This isn't a game.'

'I know,' Bram said.

Now that reality was hurtling towards her in the shape of a carriage, her good feelings towards the mask faded. She didn't want to actually take part in another hold-up. They were scary and dangerous and her smug older sister would see how utterly useless she was. The Big Top was still looming in her mind's eye, reminding her of just how much she'd lost, of how risky the world could be. And even though she knew the poor needed her help, Bram still didn't want to rob anyone.

'I don't want to be Diamond Jack,' she said, close to tears.

'Too late.' Charlie nodded at the blur of horses and the gilded carriage hurtling towards them.

'For goodness' sake,' Lena said, grabbing Bram by the arms and pushing her into the safety of the trees as if she were a toddler.

Hidden behind the branches, flooded with a mixture of failure and relief, Bram watched as Agnes-the-Blade and One-Shot Charlie stood firm in the lane, squaring up to the approaching carriage.

The horses weren't slowing down.

'They're not stopping,' Bram said, her neck slicking with sweat.

Fear turned to panic as she imagined her two friends being mowed down and caught in a stampede. Beneath the glamour, she knew that Charlie's pistols were longer than his forearms and Agnes still had twigs in her hair. She just couldn't let them get hurt. And she was Diamond Jack now, leader of the Brigands. She *had* to help.

Breaking free of her sister's grip, she dashed towards One-Shot Charlie and grabbed his arm. She pulled at him just as the horses broke into the tree tunnel. 'Come on,' she cried.

But Charlie wouldn't budge. Instead, he aimed his guns at the branches above and released two ear-splitting shots. At the same time, Agnes-the-Blade sent a small axe spinning into the trees, which found its target with a sharp thwack, sending a branch tumbling to the path below. An explosion of leaves and dirt caused the horses to skid to a halt; the coachman heaved against the reins from his place atop the carriage.

'Whoa,' he called. 'Whoa there.'

Bram couldn't help but think of the poor passengers in the carriage, thrown forward from their seats and terrified for their lives. She hated that helping the villagers meant scaring and stealing from others.

Agnes leapt over the branch in one easy stride. 'Stand and deliver,' she roared as she heaved open the carriage door.

Bram heard the excited gasps of the passengers: *It's Agnes-the-Blade. She's our favourite outlaw.*

'Your money or your life,' Charlie shouted as he circled the other side of the carriage, smoking gun pointing at the carriage window.

It's One-Shot Charlie. Quick, get his autograph.

Bram wondered if being held up by the Brigands was really such a terrifying experience. Isabel hadn't been scared either. Then, she heard sobbing. Someone *was* terrified. At first, she thought it was a passenger, then she noticed the quiver of the horse's reins as the teary coachman sucked in mouthfuls of air.

'It's OK, I'm not going to hurt you,' she said.

His black hair and dark cape reminded her of a crow.

'Don't shoot me.' His voice was a moan as he cowered inside his cape. '*Please* don't shoot.'

'I'm not going to shoot you,' she said. 'I haven't even got a gun.' She raised her hands so he could see.

The coachman pointed to the stick gun in her apron string. 'Yes you have.'

'What? This?' She pulled the sticks free. 'No, no, it's just a toy. My friend gave it to me.'

She realized that, in the panic and darkness, he must have mistaken the stick gun for a real gun, so she waved it around, demonstrating it was completely harmless. He began shrieking, hiding his head inside his cloak.

The horses shifted uneasily between their hooves, baring their teeth and snorting.

Agnes, who had been collecting coins and jewellery from the passengers, leant back and whistled. 'Oi, Jack, you're scaring the horses. Cut it out.'

'Is that Diamond Jack?' a voice called from inside the carriage. 'Oh, do your thing, Jack. Do your thing.'

Ignoring the request, Bram raised the stick gun. 'I'm just trying to calm the coachman down.'

'Where did you get that?' Agnes said, alarmed.

'Your sister's going to kill me.'

The coachman sniffed. 'With all respect, Diamond Jack, sir, how will aiming a pistol at my head calm me down?'

'It's just a couple of sticks,' she said, confused.

He peered from the folds of his cloak. 'As I live and breathe, that ain't no stick.' The whites of his eyes were perfect loops in the darkness.

Bram's jaw fell. The coachman really did see a gun and not a shoddy, makeshift toy. The stick must have been absorbed into the glamour. Just as her apron looked like a velvet jacket, her stick looked like a pistol.

She giggled in excitement and angled the sticks at a nearby tree trunk, pretending to pull the trigger, wondering if the glamour would stretch as far as making a loud noise. There was no gunshot and she bit her lip, deep in thought.

Without warning, there was a rush of movement, a loud cry, followed by a flash of silver whizzing past her head. *Swoosh. Thunk.* Bram's breath stuck in her lungs and she turned to see a slim pistol in the coachman's hand, the same hand that was now pinned to the wood of the carriage by a perfectly aimed knife through his shirt sleeve.

Lena blazed on to the path, another blade poised, ready to fling, eyes flashing. 'You get that gun away from my sister,' she screamed.

Confused, the coachman tossed his weapon at Lena's feet. 'Sorry, miss.'

Bram was still figuring out what just happened, when Lena hauled her into the trees.

'How could you be so stupid?' Her face was red even in the dimness, her voice strained with anger. 'If I hadn't been here, that coachman would have shot you. You never take your eye off a target. Never. The glamour isn't some magical armour, it's just an illusion. You're still Bramble and you can still die.'

Bram blinked away hot tears. She felt so stupid, so ashamed. She may have looked like a highwayman, but she was still just a clueless kid who worked in a shop.

'I'm sorry,' she whispered. 'I was just trying to help.'

'Just take off that wretched mask.' Lena's fingers curled around the fabric of the disguise, scratching and pinching in the process.

Crestfallen, Bram allowed Lena to grapple her face.

The carriage door slammed, the branch swished as it was dragged from the path, and the horses snorted and thundered away, taking the snivelling coachman with them.

At least the hold-up is over and nobody was harmed, Bram thought.

Lena continued to tussle with the mask. 'Have you glued it on?' Her voice peaked in frustration and she accidentally yanked a lock of Bram's hair.

'It keeps getting stuck,' Bram replied, trying to ease the fabric from the back of her head. 'I tried to tell you, remember?'

Agnes-the-Blade and One-Shot Charlie ran into the trees, their hands overflowing with dazzling jewels, their faces plastered with breathless smiles.

'That was a good haul,' Charlie said. 'We can feed a village for a month with all those coins.'

'You can't beat an unexpected hold-up,' Agnes said with a laugh.

Finally admitting defeat, Lena released Bram's face and flounced over to the nearest tree, which she kicked in frustration. Leaves showered around her.

'What's that about?' Agnes asked, stuffing the bounty into her pockets.

Lena turned, her face swollen with rage. 'Bram here nearly got shot.'

Charlie scratched his beard. 'We've all nearly been shot, Lena. It goes with the job.'

For a moment, Bram thought her sister was going to cry, but instead she opened the duffel bags and began rummaging through them.

'I don't want to talk about it any more,' Lena snapped, chucking each of the Brigands a leaf-coated jumper. 'We need to hide before Mickey and his gang arrive.' She pointed upwards and Bram could just make out pockets of the indigo night sky through the leaves.

'Where did you get the gun?' Agnes asked, gesturing to the toy in Bram's hand.

'Oh, it's not real,' Bram replied. 'It's just a couple of sticks and some twine that Ernest got from a girl in the village. The glamour must work on weapons too.'

'It's been known to happen,' Charlie said. 'It's handy.'

'It's not handy, Chuck,' Lena said. 'It's dangerous. The coachman only shot her because he was scared. Guns attract guns.'

'So why have you got one?' Charlie said, pointing to Lena's holster.

Lena made a noise halfway between a growl and a

scream. 'Just take off those stupid masks and get into your camouflage gear. The Rippers will be here soon.'

It was a strange sight, Bram decided, watching her sister boss two armed highwaymen around, but they did as she said, and before long Agnes-the-Blade and One-Shot Charlie were a couple of kids wriggling into forest-covered clothes.

'What should *I* do?' Bram asked, the mask still plastered to her face.

Lena glared at her. 'Just keep pulling at it.'

After changing into their camouflage clothes and smearing dirt on to their faces, Lena and Agnes disappeared up two of the tallest trees, while Bram, who'd never been much good at climbing, and Charlie, whose limbs were too short to reach the lower branches, hid in a nearby bush. Twigs pricked Bram's skin and the scent of earth and damp grass filled her nose.

Night fell and the Crooked Woods came alive. Owls hooted, badgers grunted, insects hummed. The moon provided just enough light that Bram could make out Charlie beside her. She was just beginning to feel sleepy when she heard a low snuffling sound followed by the crunch of feet against dirt.

'Mickey?' she mouthed at Charlie.

Charlie nodded, his leaf-encrusted hat dancing on his head. Flattening herself to the forest floor, Bram felt her muscles tighten, as taut as a bow. The sound of a twig snapping invaded her ears and caused her heart to climb into her throat.

Something touched her leg and Bram held back a scream. She whipped her feet away, desperately trying to escape the monster in the dark, be it Mickey, Connie, Nines or all three.

It didn't work.

The sharp prick of nails scraped her thigh, her hip, her back . . .

Only when a wet tongue licked her cheek did she realize the monster was Bertie.

'Oh, Bertie,' she giggled, sitting up and tickling his head. 'You scared the life out of me.'

Charlie stifled a laugh. 'He must have followed us.'

The terrier released a happy yip and Bram hushed him, gently touching his muzzle and lowering her face to his.

'We need to be really quiet, Bertie-boos,' she whispered.

His damp nose slid against her cheek and he nibbled her ear.

'Not now, Bertie,' she said, chuckling and trying to hold him still.

He let out a playful growl and licked her cheek again. His nose pushed beneath her mask.

Bram didn't even consider that the mask could come loose – only a few minutes ago it had been clamped firmly to her head – yet at Bertie's touch, the cloth fell from her face and plopped on to his muzzle. Charlie hiccupped back a laugh and Bertie began to shake as if caught in the rain, but rather than fling it free, the mask settled around his eyes so it really did look like he was about to shout, *Stand and deliver*.

Charlie clutched his sides to stop himself laughing any louder.

'Shush!' came a hiss from up high.

Bram knew they were being too noisy, but after nearly getting shot, Lena's outburst, and mistaking Bertie for Mickey, all of her nervous energy turned into laughter and she guffawed hopelessly into her palms.

'Be quiet,' Lena called.

Why is it the harder you try not to laugh, the funnier it seems? Bram thought.

Bertie tilted his head, ears pricked.

'Quick, get the mask,' Charlie spluttered. 'The last

thing we need is Bertie becoming a highwayman. Could you imagine?'

'Don't worry.' Bram felt the laughter ease its grip as she managed to catch a breath. 'If the mask won't work for Lena and Ernest, it won't work for Bertie.'

'Maybe it's different for dogs,' he replied.

'It only works for me.'

'Even if you said, "*Mask, work for Bertie*"?' Charlie said, his mouth drawn in a cheeky grin.

Bram sighed away the remnants of her giggling fit. 'Even if I said, "*Mask, work for Bertie*",' she said.

As soon as the words left her lips, Bertie vanished and a fully grown highwayman appeared on Bram's lap. Crimson mask, navy jacket, dark hair, square jaw. Diamond Jack cocked his head and twitched his nose.

'Yap!' Jack shouted, before trying to lick her face.

CHAPTER
22

'Aargh!' Bram jumped to her feet, tearing through the branches above and causing the highwayman to tumble to the floor.

'Oh my goodness,' Charlie said. 'Bertie is Diamond Jack.'

The highwayman rolled on to his back, flipped on to his front, then scampered away on his hands and knees, pausing to sniff a nearby tree.

'How on earth did that happen?' Bram asked.

Charlie backed out of the bush. 'I don't know.'

'Has he got . . . dog ears?' Bram said, pointing at the

two perfectly tufted ears that poked from Jack's floppy hair.

'And a tail,' Charlie said with a giggle.

Sure enough, Bertie's long, scrappy tail emerged from Jack's bottom, wagging against the forest floor, sending soil and dead leaves flying.

'It must be a bit like my necklace and eye colour,' Bram said. 'Whatever's inside the wearer's heart shines through the glamour.'

Diamond Jack, still crouched on his hands and knees, began cocking his leg against a nearby tree. The sound of pee hitting bark drifted towards them.

'We need to get the mask back,' Charlie said, swallowing a chuckle. 'Before the Rippers arrive.'

'Here, boy,' Bram whispered, arms outstretched. 'Here, boy. Come to Bramble. Good doggy.'

Diamond Jack sat next to the steaming damp patch, threw back his head and barked.

A furious whisper came from Lena above. 'What is going on down there?'

'Nothing,' Bram said. 'Bertie followed us here.'

'Well, keep him quiet,' Lena hissed. 'Mickey and his gang will be here any moment.'

'Yeah, cut it out,' Agnes said.

Diamond Jack began scratching his dog ear with his foot, sending his dark floppy hair whirling about his face. Charlie launched himself on top of the itchy outlaw. But Jack was faster and whipped to the side, landing on all fours and yapping excitedly.

Charlie fell on his bottom and winced. 'The mask worked on Bertie when you told it to. Maybe it follows orders. Try telling it to stop.'

'Mask, stop working for Bertie,' Bram said, her voice a shrill warble.

Diamond Jack began chasing his tail, his blue velvet jacket flaring and his hair bouncing. If Mickey and his gang turned up now, Bertie wouldn't stand a chance. She had to do something. Watching the terrier-turned-highwayman, she wished she had a sausage to coax him with. That's when she remembered the soggy velvet pouch that Ernest had given her back at the hideaway.

Tearing it from her apron pocket, she tipped the contents on to her palm.

A lump of cold pheasant.

'I can hear horses,' Lena hissed. 'Stop messing around and be quiet.'

Bram froze and listened. The thud of hooves in the distance.

Her hands shaking, Bram held out the offering. 'Here, Bertie-boos. Good doggy.'

Diamond Jack shoved his bottom in the air, stretched his arms into the ground, then, shuffling forward on his hands and knees, snaffled the pheasant from her palm.

'Please don't stick,' she whispered as she pulled the mask from the mop of dark hair with her spare hand. It slipped away with ease. In an instant, Diamond Jack disappeared and a hairy dog chewing on a lump of cold bird appeared in his place.

'Quickly,' Charlie whispered.

Whisking Bertie into her arms, Bram dived back into the bush beside Charlie.

She was just in time; through the mat of leaves, she saw hooves shining on the path beyond.

The Rippers had arrived.

CHAPTER 23

Peering through the branches, Bram could just make out the outline of the Rippers. Adrenalin burst through her veins. She gripped Bertie a little tighter, feeling grateful for the comfort of his fur and willing him not to bark.

'Where is he then?' Connie said, jumping from her horse. Her knives rattled and her braid flashed silver beneath the moon. 'Where's the Diamond?'

A cruel sneer of a voice cut the black night, setting Bram's head spinning with fear. It was Mickey. 'I told him the usual spot.'

'He'll be 'ere soon.' The voice was gravel and too much salt, and Bram remembered hearing it that day at the emporium, coming from the man she couldn't see.

Leaning forward, she tried to get a better look. The first thing that struck her was his size, as he was even larger than Mickey, causing his poor horse to sag beneath his weight. Next she noticed his pale skin, rising from his black stubble and tightening over his head so it shone in the night. Indeed the only other thing visible against his dark clothes were his hands, as pallid and large as stone flags.

He slid from his horse with a loud thunk and stomped up and down the path, his fist thumping into his palm as if craving something to punch. Clinging to Bertie, Bram tried not to think about Lena and Agnes up in the treetops.

Connie kicked a pebble from her path. 'Will you stop with all that thumping, Nines. It's like a dripping tap. Drives me mad.'

Nines turned, eyes gleaming. 'Shut it.' He returned to watching the trees. 'Well, he can't like the old man that much if he don't even turn up.'

'*Doesn't* even show up,' Connie said. 'Learn to speak.'

'Shut it.' His fist quickened against his palm.

Casually, she ran a finger down the handle of her largest blade, just like she'd done back at the emporium. 'Do you *want* to lose another digit?'

'I can still throttle you with eight.'

With a shudder, Bram thought how hard it must be to slice through one of those fingers – they were as thick as broom handles.

'Nines, Cutthroat, that's quite enough,' Mickey said. 'The Diamond's got an hour, then we head back to the lair.'

'Aye, boss,' they grumbled.

'Try not to kill each other.'

'Aye, boss.'

'And stay alert – if a carriage comes by, we may as well rob it.'

Bertie whimpered and Bram lowered her head to shush him. At the exact same time, Charlie spun towards the noise, knocking his head into hers so that a noisy breath pushed from her lips: *Ooph!*

Mickey wheeled towards them. 'What was that?'

Bram froze, her heart thumping in her throat.

'It were just the wind,' Nines said.

Connie scoffed. 'You've been punched too many

times in the ears, I reckon. Wind doesn't whimper and it doesn't say "ooph".

'It could be the Diamond,' Mickey said, pulling a flintlock pistol from the holster on his hip.

The steps of the Rippers approached. Bram could hear the jangle of Connie's knives and the click of a safety being removed. She forced down a gasp as the leaves above her head began to shake.

A large, pale hand curled around a branch only inches from her head.

Instead of an index finger there was a shiny nub of healed skin.

CHAPTER 24

Nearby, something fell from the trees – a stone or a pine cone.

The hand slinked away from the branch above.

'He's over there,' Connie said, spinning away.

Another sound as something pinged off a tree trunk then hit the ground. The Rippers moved towards the noise. Agnes and Lena must have carefully aimed tiny missiles from their positions in the tree-tops. *Thank you, Lena and Agnes*, Bram thought.

But the Rippers weren't the only ones drawn to

the noise: Bertie came to life, jumping from Bram's lap and shimmying through the branches. Bram mouthed the word 'no', her hands swiping after him. But it was no use. The little terrier had caught up with the Rippers, his bark echoing through the Crooked Woods.

Connie laughed. 'It's just a mangy little mutt.'

Bertie's hackles rose and he released a low growl.

Nines grunted. 'He's an ugly little grub, ain't he?'

'Shall I kill it?' Connie asked, brandishing a knife.

Charlie reached for his pistol, and Bram realized she was clenching her fists, ready for action even though she'd never fought in her life.

Mickey kissed his teeth. 'No point getting blood on your best knife, Cutthroat.'

'Well, let's shoot it then,' Nines said, pulling a pistol from his belt.

'Idiot!' Mickey said. 'The gunshot might scare the Diamond away.'

'Sorry, boss,' Nines said, his face glum as he put his gun away.

A brutal smile touched Mickey's thin lips. He pulled back his foot and let it swing at the terrier with all his force.

A scream rose up Bram's throat, just as Charlie's hand clamped over her mouth and Bertie darted to the side, dodging the boot and burrowing into a nearby bush.

'Get him, boss,' Nines roared.

Mickey laughed. 'Let him go. We've got bigger mutts to catch.'

Tears of relief gathered in Bram's eyes as she heard Bertie bound through the forest, away from the Rippers, their weapons and their swinging boots. *Hopefully he's heading back to our hideaway*, she thought, *back to roasted rabbit and tummy rubs*.

The next hour was the longest of Bram's life, and their den was starting to feel less like a den and more like a prison cell, the branches becoming metal bars and the soft mulchy floor as cold as concrete. She could only imagine how uncomfortable Lena and Agnes must be, clinging to tree branches.

Finally, Nines spoke from his position sitting on an upended tree root. 'He ain't coming.'

'*Isn't* coming,' Connie said, standing and brushing the dirt from her jacket. 'Idiotic brute.'

'Shut it,' Nines spat.

Mickey, who'd been leaning against a tree trunk,

straightened up and cracked his knuckles. 'Let's head back to the lair. Get some sleep.'

The trio began untethering their rides from a nearby branch.

Bram's mind turned to Dusty; she hoped her faithful steed wasn't too scared of the Crooked Woods whilst huddled with the other horses. Silently, she promised to give her some extra apples when this ordeal was over.

Nines adjusted his saddle. 'Can we finally kill the old man?' he asked.

Bram's heart spiralled out of control. *Don't kill Grandpa*, she thought. *Please, not Grandpa.*

'Seems fair,' Connie said, jumping on to her horse. 'The Diamond knew the deal. No Jack, no old man.' She mimed slitting her own throat.

The image of her beloved grandfather all alone on the floor of some grotty lair landed in Bram's mind like an arrow. What was the point in following the outlaws if Grandpa was dead when they finally reached him? She had to do something. Her head reeling, she barely noticed her numb fingers reaching towards the mask in her apron pocket.

'Bram, what are you doing?' Charlie whispered.

'You heard them. No Jack, no Grandpa,' she said, fixing the mask to her face.

Whoosh. Fizz.

She clenched her muscles, readying herself to spring from the bush.

But Charlie grabbed her shoulders. 'Wait,' he mouthed.

She paused, just long enough to hear Mickey say, 'Tell me, Nines, have you ever been fishing?'

'Fishing? Course I 'ave, boss. Why d'ya ask?'

'And you popped a maggot on to the hook before dangling it into the water?'

'Yeah,' Nines replied.

Mickey sighed. 'So when you didn't get a bite, did you try again, or did you squash the maggot?'

'I tried again, boss. But what's that got to do with Jack and the old man?'

Connie laughed. 'You seriously don't see where he's going with this?'

'Shut it,' Nines said.

'So that's what we're going to do,' Mickey said, mounting his ride and heading on to the path so the moonlight hit his skull face. 'We're going to try again. We'll leave another note telling him to meet us on a different night.'

'Eh?' Nines said, following after Mickey. 'Are we going fishing afterwards?'

Bram could practically hear Connie rolling her eyes as she too set off down the path.

'It's a *metaphor*,' Connie said. 'The old man is the maggot and Diamond Jack is the fish. If we squash the maggot, we never catch the fish. Idiot.'

'But Diamond Jack ain't a fish,' Nines said.

As their voices faded into the dark, Bram sank back into the bush, tears of relief threatening to spill down her face. But she didn't have time to cry, as Charlie was already hoisting her up.

'Come on,' he hissed. 'Or we'll lose them.'

Standing, she tried to pull the mask free. It held tight.

'Of course you're stuck,' she hissed. Then she remembered: the mask followed orders. 'Mask, get off my face,' she said, but it didn't budge, not even with the sharpest of tugs.

'Interesting,' Charlie said. 'You can only order it to work for someone else.'

'It isn't interesting, it's annoying,' Bram said.

He grinned. 'You do remind me of your sister sometimes.'

Before she could object, Lena and Agnes dropped from their hiding places in the trees.

'Bramble Browning, take off that mask at once,' Lena hissed. She had leaves in her hair and a smudge of dirt on her cheek.

'I can't, it's stuck,' Bram replied.

'Oh, for the love of Queen Georgina,' she muttered. 'We're stuck with the worst Diamond Jack in the history of the queendom.'

Anger and hurt flared in Bram's stomach, but there wasn't time to argue. They had to find Grandpa. So they began following the Rippers, jogging through the forest, tracking the edge of the dirt lane, dodging branches and hopping over tree roots, moving as quietly as possible.

The Rippers turned into the woodland on the other side of the path. The thick knit of trees slowed them down, allowing the Brigands to follow them with ease. Bram's hands stung from the constant scrape of twigs and her cheeks throbbed from the slap of leaves. Just as she was beginning to wonder if they would ever reach the lair, the Rippers paused at a jagged cliff that reared above the trees like a giant shard of ice.

Then, without warning, Mickey vanished. Bram

blinked quickly. One second he was there, flexing his muscles, and then he wasn't. Next to disappear was Nines, followed by Connie.

Squinting through the leaves, Bram picked out the mouth of a cave, a black yawn slashed into the rock.

'The Rippers' lair,' Lena said, her voice low. 'Finally.'

Grandpa, Bram thought, daring to hope she would see him soon.

'A cave!' Agnes said. 'With all they've stolen I assumed they would live somewhere fancy.'

Bram nodded. 'It makes the hideaway look like a mansion.'

'The hideaway *is* a mansion,' Charlie said, his voice proud. 'It just gets a bit cold in the winter.'

'A bit?' Agnes said with a wink.

Lena leant forward and took Bram's hands. 'It's going to be all right now.'

'Thanks, Lena,' she replied. And she couldn't help but wonder if it was strange for her sister to comfort a fully grown highwayman.

'Now we wait,' Lena said, crossing her arms against the chill. 'And when the Rippers leave, we get Grandpa.'

Just then, an animal shot from the undergrowth. At first, Bram thought it was a fox or a badger, then she realized it was Bertie, wagging his tail and panting with excitement.

'He's followed us again,' she said, exasperated.

'Shoo, Bertie, go home,' Charlie said.

Bertie sat on the leaf-strewn forest floor and whimpered.

'Go find Ernest,' Bram said. 'He's got more pheasant.'

The terrier tipped his whiskered face in understanding, then darted back into the trees.

'Just what we need,' Lena said, rolling her eyes. 'A yappy dog following us around.'

Bram had the urge to defend Bertie, but she simply bit her lip.

After agreeing to take it in turns to sleep and keep watch, Lena took up post while Bram, Agnes and Charlie snuggled into the undergrowth, keen to rest their eyes. Agnes began to snore almost immediately, whereas Charlie propped himself on his elbow, his eyelids drooping as he stifled a yawn.

'Are you going to tell Lena about what happened with Bertie and the mask?' Charlie whispered.

Bram fidgeted with the fabric against her face. It still wouldn't budge. Should she tell Lena what had happened? After all, if she could order the mask to work for Bertie, she could order it to work for Lena. And Lena was a much better highwayman than her.

And yet . . .

'I don't know,' Bram replied. 'I think it was just a fluke it worked for Bertie. Don't you?'

'Maybe.'

Charlie didn't look too sure. And Bram didn't blame him. The truth was, she didn't want to give the mask to Lena – she liked the fact the mask had chosen her. And whilst being a highwayman scared her, something about it excited and thrilled her too. Besides, she couldn't bear to see the smug look on Lena's face if she got the mask back again. Those hurtful words pulsed in her head: *We're stuck with the worst Diamond Jack in the history of the queendom.* Bram simply couldn't let Lena be Diamond Jack again. Not after saying *that*.

A sharp hiss pulled her from her thoughts. 'They're leaving.'

It was Lena.

The fear came flooding back into sharp focus. 'Why would they leave so soon?' Bram asked.

Something didn't feel right. It was just too easy.

'Don't complain,' Agnes said, sitting up and rubbing her cheeks. Pulling her purple mask over her mass of curls, she immediately changed into Agnes-the-Blade.

'Really?' Lena said. 'You think wearing your mask into the lair is a good idea?'

'What difference does it make?' Agnes replied. 'The Rippers have gone now. Anyway, Bram's wearing hers.'

'Only because it won't come off,' Lena said.

Agnes shrugged. 'What can I say? It makes me feel stronger.'

Bram understood what Agnes meant. Although she felt like a fraud wearing the mask, she also felt snippets of power, glimpses of courage. She would never have pulled Charlie from the path of the carriage if she weren't Diamond Jack, nor would she have been ready to jump out at the Rippers when they were trying to hurt Bertie, or when Connie wanted to kill Grandpa.

Charlie grinned. 'We're doing magic. Awesome.' He swapped his hat for his blue mask and was instantly replaced by a six-foot bearded outlaw.

'Oh, great,' Lena muttered. 'Now I'm the only one without a mask.'

'And now you sound like Ernest,' Agnes said, smiling.

Together, they watched as the Rippers rode back into the woods.

'Where are they going?' Bram asked.

Charlie shrugged. 'Probably on a hold-up.'

'No rest for the wicked,' Agnes said, tucking a black curl behind her ear.

The friends waited until they were gone and after what felt like forever, Lena finally hissed, 'OK, it's safe. Let's go.'

Stepping into the cave was like falling down a deep hole, not knowing how long the darkness stretched, all the while imagining the nightmares that lurked at the bottom. But after a few steps, Bram could see a light flickering in the distance, casting spidery shadows across the rock of the passageway.

'Grandpa?' Bram called.

A muffled reply came from the end of the corridor.

Grandpa!

A rush of joy fuelled her tired legs and Bram found she was sprinting, knocking against the rough stone and not caring when it scraped her arms.

'Bramble, wait,' Lena said.

But Bram simply quickened, stopping only when she entered a large chamber. Water dripped from the walls and candles sprouted around the edge of the floor.

And there in the middle of the room, tied to a chair, mouth bound shut with cloth, was Grandpa.

Bram's heart swelled with love and happiness.

'Grandpa!' She reached him in two giant steps, threw her arms around him and almost knocked his chair to the ground. 'It's me, Bramble,' she said, aware she looked like Diamond Jack.

Charlie's voice filled the room. 'This doesn't look like a lair.'

Bram only part-heard, she was too busy trying to remove the gag from Grandpa's mouth. The Rippers had tied it so tight it dug into the corners of his lips and left pink marks on his skin. Lena joined her and together they began loosening the knot at the back of his head. All the while, Grandpa's blue eyes were wide and dancing, his words a string of grunts that stumbled on the cloth in his mouth.

He was trying to tell them something.

'What is it, Grandpa?' Bram asked.

He began thumping his feet against the ground and straining against his ropes, his desperation climbing. The knot began to loosen beneath Bram's frantic hands, and Lena moved to his front, trying to ease the rag from his mouth.

Circling the cave, Agnes sucked air over her teeth. 'You're right, Chuck, this isn't a lair. There's no furniture or food or *anything*. Something isn't right.'

Finally, the knot unwound and the gag came free in Lena's hands.

Grandpa gulped down a mouthful of air, threw back his head and shouted, 'It's a trap. A trap. The Rippers only pretended to leave.'

His words bounced around the stone walls so they were all that Bram could hear.

She wanted to scream, to cry, wanted to sweep Grandpa into her arms and run and run and run until they were home and safe, until the Crooked Woods became no more than a dark memory. But before she could do anything, a cold, cruel voice sliced through the gloom.

'Diamond Jack,' Mickey said. 'So good of you to show up.'

She turned to see the Rippers blocking the only exit with their muscles, their weapons and their wicked smiles.

CHAPTER
25

'Put your weapons on the ground,' Connie shouted, her hands loaded with two angry knives.

The Brigands didn't stand a chance – just the smallest of movements would make them attack, and the Rippers didn't shoot to miss.

They shot to kill.

Metal clattered against the stone floor as Agnes-the-Blade, One-Shot Charlie and Lena emptied their holsters.

'Don't be shy, Agnes.' Connie pointed at the

crossing leather straps of knives on Agnes's chest.

'I haven't taken these off in over a year,' Agnes grumbled as she pulled the belts over her head and chucked them at Connie's feet.

'And the pockets,' Connie said.

Agnes and Charlie threw the loot they'd gathered from the earlier hold-up on to the ground. Jewellery and coins skidded across the stone. Charlie sighed and Bram knew he was thinking about all the villagers he was no longer able to help.

Nines gathered all of the weapons and treasure into a linen sack, pausing only to admire one of Charlie's pistols and tuck it into his boot.

'Hey,' Charlie said. 'That's mine.'

'Finders sleepers,' Nines said.

Connie rolled her eyes and swapped her own weapons belt for Agnes's. 'You're so embarrassing, Nines. It's finders *keepers*.'

'Shut it,' Nines said.

'Stop bickering,' Mickey growled. He trained a flintlock pistol on Bram's chest. His gaze intensified and his eyes became two black dashes. 'Hello, Diamond,' he said, his voice a snarl.

She wanted to say something clever, something

brave, but her mouth felt like it had been stuffed with cardboard.

Mickey smirked. 'Don't tell me that the great Diamond Jack is lost for words?'

Bram swallowed.

His smirk grew and he turned his attention to the other prisoners. 'Well, well, well. It's my lucky day. With just one maggot I've caught three fish – Diamond Jack, One-Shot Charlie and Agnes-the-Blade. Who'd have thought the notorious Brigands would care so much about some crumbly old man.'

You're the maggot, Bram wanted to shout, but her voice failed her entirely.

Grandpa simply chuckled. 'Nothing wrong with being crumbly. Ask my cookies.'

Mickey looked like he ate bullets and steel, not biscuits. But Bram took comfort from the fact that Grandpa sounded strong and unharmed.

'And who's this?' Mickey said, pointing at Lena with the nose of his gun.

'I'm your worst nightmare,' Lena replied, her voice low and steady. 'And I give it five minutes before you're begging for mercy.'

Bram's insides churned with shame. Lena was so

brave. So sure of herself. Bram was struggling to draw breath, and yet here was Lena hurling threats. Maybe Bram had jumped into the path of the carriage, and maybe she'd been ready to save Bertie and Grandpa, but when things got really tough, she folded as easily as paper.

As soon as the scarlet mask came free, she'd order it to work for Lena, she decided. Looking like Diamond Jack was no use to Grandpa, no use to *anyone*, if she couldn't behave like Diamond Jack.

Mickey laughed. 'Begging for mercy, you say? Somehow I doubt that, *sweetheart*.'

'I still don't get the fish thing,' Nines said.

'I told you, it's a *metaphor*,' Connie snapped.

Nines nodded, though his pale forehead creased with confusion. 'So will the Princess Regent be pleased we're having fish for tea?'

'Oh yes,' Mickey said. 'Princess Lavinia will be thrilled. It's practically a banquet.'

Bram was pretty sure that Nines still thought they were actually having fish for tea.

'Line up and turn round,' Connie shouted, raising her knives. 'And put your hands behind your backs.'

As she turned, Bram surveyed the cave, desperately

looking for a solution: a hidden exit, a box of secret weapons, anything they could use to help, but there was nothing but a few useless candles. She bit back a frustrated cry. They'd been so close. *At least they won't hurt Grandpa now they've got Jack*, she thought. Though judging from Mickey's sinister glare, even that wasn't a given.

Reluctantly, her friends faced the back of the cave so Nines and Connie could move between them, looping rope around their wrists and legs. Shadows spun across the walls of the chamber as the candles danced to their movement. The smell of smoke, body odour and damp rock left Bram feeling queasy. The other end of the ropes were attached to metal hoops that had been nailed to the wall so there was no leaving the cave. Nines jerked the cords around Bram's hands, burning her skin and causing a whimper of pain to escape from her mouth.

He laughed. 'Is the great Diamond Jack a scaredy mouse?'

'Scaredy *cat*,' Connie said.

Nines spun Bram around. 'What have we got 'ere?' He raised an eyebrow, before bellowing, 'Cutthroat. You missed one.'

'What?' Connie said.

'Diamond's still got his pistol. I can see the hilt.'

With a flash of panic, Bram remembered she was still carrying the stick gun. Before she could even begin to explain, Connie had stormed towards her, blade raised and blonde plait swaying like a white viper.

'Thought you could sneak one past me, did you, Diamond?'

Up close, Bram could finally make out her features beneath the tricorn hat – it was a face that knew only how to scowl.

In a whir of movement, Connie ripped the fake pistol from Bram's apron string and slung it on the ground.

Nines picked it up and laughed. 'My bad! It's just a toy.'

'Oh, do be quiet, Nines,' Connie said, her eyes still glued to Bram.

'No, really,' Nines said. 'The Diamond's carrying a fake.' He aimed it at Connie and pretended to shoot. 'Pow, pow, you're dead. Nines has shot you in the head.'

Spinning, Connie hurled a blade through the air and knocked the toy straight from Nines's fingers.

Bram gawped at the speed at which Connie's hands could move.

'Ouch,' Nines said, cradling his hand. 'You nearly stuck me again.'

Mickey picked up the fake pistol. 'Nines is right, Cutthroat. This gun isn't real.'

The Brigands exchanged a worried glance.

Connie's fists clenched. 'You always take his side, boss.' She stamped her foot, her plait flicked, and for a brief moment, Bram thought the terrifying highwayman looked like a spoiled child having a tantrum.

'Not true,' Nines grumbled. 'You're definitely his favourite.'

Mickey's face turned so red he looked like a flaming skull. 'Be quiet. You're like a couple of squabbling brats.' Skilfully, he tossed the stick gun at Connie, who swiped it from the air and gasped.

'Well, I'll be damned,' she said. 'I could have sworn it was real.'

'Perhaps you're losing your touch, Cutthroat,' Mickey said with a sneer. 'Maybe I should get a new knife thrower.' He turned to Agnes. 'Well, Agnes-the-Blade? There's an opening on the winning team if you're interested.'

'Not a chance,' she growled.

'Like I'd want you anyway,' he said, his sneer broadening. 'You support that pathetic joke of a queen – Queen Georgina.'

'Don't you dare talk about the one true queen like that.' Agnes tried to lunge at him, only to fall on the floor with a crack now her ankles were bound together.

'Boss!' Connie shouted. 'You need to look at this.'

'Not now,' Mickey said, as he loomed over a writhing Agnes, foot drawn back and ready to kick.

'Seriously, boss,' Connie said, 'you need to see this.'

'What is it?' Mickey roared, spit flying from his lips.

At least he's lowered his foot, Bram thought with a wave of relief.

When Mickey looked at Connie, the anger left his face and was replaced by an expression of alarm.

Bram followed his line of sight, her breath sputtering. Just beside her stomach, she saw the stick gun dangling from Connie's fingers, and judging from everyone's expressions, it wasn't a toy any more, it was real. Then, very slowly, as Connie moved it away from Bram, a collective gasp echoed around the chamber. Bram could only imagine what they all could see: a metal pistol transforming back into sticks.

'Oh no,' Lena murmured.

Mickey's look of alarm turned into a slow, sick laugh. 'I can smell something, Cutthroat,' he said. 'What about you?'

'Aye, boss,' she said. 'And it smells pretty strong, I reckon.'

'Sorry,' Nines said, fanning a hand at his rear end.

Ignoring him, Mickey stroked the underbelly of his chin with a knife. 'The whole cave stinks of it,' he said.

Connie nodded. '*Reeks* of it, boss.'

Nines sniffed his pits. 'I had a bath a month back, I swear.'

Mickey sauntered towards Bram, his knife dancing between his fingers. 'Magic,' he said. 'I can smell magic.'

CHAPTER
26

'I don't know what you're talking about,' Bram said.

'Oh, really?' Mickey rested the point of his blade against her throat. A sharp needle of pain pierced her skin and panic flooded her system; it was all she could do not to faint.

'Just tell me what's going on, Diamond.' Mickey's breath smelt of rotting meat. 'Are you in league with a witch? A warlock?'

Lena scoffed. 'Magic died out years ago. Everyone knows that, you idiot!'

Nines shoved Lena between the shoulder blades

with the butt of his pistol, sending her sprawling on to the stone floor beside Agnes.

'Lena!' Grandpa said as he fought helplessly against his bindings.

Bram fought the urge to rush to her, the tip of Mickey's blade still needling her skin.

Mickey leant forward so that his nose almost touched Bram's own. 'Or maybe *you're* the sorcerer,' he said. 'And here everyone thought you were so noble, such a good highwayman, when really, it was all magic.'

'Diamond Jack *is* a good highwayman,' Lena spat.

'It only works on weapons,' Bram garbled, desperate to save Lena from another assault. 'The enchantment only works on weapons.'

'Go on,' Mickey said.

'I've got this gift that . . . that makes sticks look like weapons when I hold them.'

Mickey studied her with interest. His breath was hot and damp and she tried not to wince. He was so close she could see every sparse lash around his black eyes.

'And why should I believe a word that comes out of your mouth, wizard?' He smiled a curious smile. 'Turns out I've always wanted to meet a sorcerer. The ultimate power! Let's see that face of yours, magic man.' His free hand reached towards her mask.

Her heart rate soared, her lip trembled. 'No,' she whispered, silently pleading with the mask to do its usual trick and remain plastered to her skin.

The tips of his fingers were rough as they touched her cheeks, her temples, her ears . . . And then there was just the chill of the air around her eyes as the mask slipped clean away.

CHAPTER

27

Mickey's scream was higher-pitched than that of a newborn babe's, as he leapt backwards, his face stretched with shock and fear. 'What magic is this?' he managed to croak.

The mask fluttered to the ground.

Connie, who'd dropped her knives, pulled two more from her belt and composed herself. 'Er, boss. That isn't Diamond Jack.'

'I can see that,' Mickey said, his voice shrill.

Nines slapped his own face a couple of times. 'Am I seeing things? Or is Diamond Jack a ... a ... little girl?'

Tears nipped at Bram's eyes. She snatched a quick glimpse of the scarlet mask at her feet – why hadn't it stuck to her face? Did it *want* her to get killed?

Mickey followed her line of sight. 'Oh, I see.' He picked up the red cloth and examined it. 'The *mask* is magic. It transforms you into a highwayman. Tell me I'm wrong.'

'It won't work for you,' Lena shouted from her position on the floor. 'It only works for Bramble.'

'So that's your real name,' Mickey said, peering into Bram's face. 'Well, hello, *Bramble*.'

She hated the sound of her name in his mouth, as if he had stolen something special from her, not just the mask. Pressing her lips together, she tried not to shake. She'd thought she was scared before, but now the mask was gone, she felt as if she were standing naked with a target on her forehead.

'Hey, boss,' Connie said. 'What about her friends? They're wearing masks too.'

Without a word, Mickey lunged at One-Shot Charlie, whipping the blue cloth from his face and transforming him back into a boy, just as Connie crouched beside Agnes-the-Blade and revealed her true, younger form.

'No. Way.' Connie's voice was caught somewhere between excitement and amazement as she flapped the purple mask in her hand.

Agnes battled against her ropes. 'Give that back!' she shouted. 'They're our magic masks. They belong to *us*.'

Charlie narrowed his eyes and sniffed loudly. He looked so small, especially with the leafy hat still rammed over his head.

'They're just kids,' Nines said, punching his fist against his palm. 'Not highwaymen, not even fish. Just snot-nosed kids.'

'Hey,' Charlie said, wrinkling his nose so his freckles disappeared.

Bram caught Grandpa's eye. A faint smile danced across his mouth and Bram understood that he was trying to tell her everything would be OK. She didn't believe him.

'*Three* magic masks,' Mickey said, smiling his slow, twisted smile. 'Three magic masks for three Rippers.'

Connie frowned. 'But we're already highwaymen, boss. The masks can't turn us into what we already are.'

'Think, Cutthroat, think. If they can turn three kids into highwaymen, imagine what they can do for us. We could be even bigger, even stronger. Or . . . or . . . we could look like the Brigands – defenders of the one true queen. Imagine what we could get away with if we looked like Diamond Jack, Agnes-the-Blade and One-Shot Charlie. Imagine the damage we could do.'

Connie nodded, her face curving into a thin smile. 'You're a genius, boss.' She passed Charlie's blue mask to Nines.

'Can I have the purple one?' Nines asked. 'It goes with the veins on me head.'

Connie gave him a stern look, then slipped off her hat and stretched out the purple cloth.

'On the count of three,' Mickey said. 'One, two, three.'

Bram knew the masks only worked for their masters, but it was still a huge relief when the three thugs tied the fabric around their heads and nothing happened.

Roaring in frustration, Mickey tore the mask off. 'Why won't they work?'

'Because you're not brave and pure of heart,' Lena said.

Mickey hurled the mask on the floor. 'No, it's

because they're useless.'

'It's all right, boss,' Nines said, removing his mask with care. 'We don't need no masks to catch Queen Georgina.'

'What?' Agnes said, her voice trembling.

'That's what we're doing tomorrow morning, ain't it, boss,' Nines said. 'Kidnapping the Queen when she travels from the hospital back to the palace. It's going to be the best hold-up *ever*.'

Bram's stomach dropped. She recalled the whispers that Queen Georgina was recovering and would soon be moved back to the palace to reclaim her throne. She just hadn't realized it would be so soon. *So that's why the mask called to me*, she thought. *The Queen really is in danger.* She shared a horrified look with her friends.

'Shut up, Nines,' Connie said, pulling the mask from her face and crumpling it into a ball. 'That's a secret.'

'It's OK,' Mickey said, shoving the scarlet mask into his back pocket. 'What can they do? They're going to be tied up here.'

Agnes strained against her ropes. 'You leave Queen Georgina alone, you snakes.'

Mickey grinned. 'Oh, we will. We'll steal her away and then we'll leave her alone, right in the middle of the ocean with a couple of bricks tied to her ankles.'

'No!' Agnes roared.

Bram felt like she'd been punched in the guts. They were going to kill Queen Georgina. That would mean Princess Lavinia would take over for good. Her power would be limitless. Not only was this awful for poor Queen Georgina, but the poorest villagers would struggle to eat and might even *starve*.

Agnes began wriggling across the floor, trying to reach the exit, but the metal hoops that secured her ropes to the wall held her firmly in place.

Grandpa began banging his feet against the floor. 'Queen Georgina's guards will stop you,' he shouted, his blue eyes filled with such determination Bram suddenly found it easy to believe he'd once been a highwayman.

'Will they?' Connie said. 'Or will they accept the bribe from the Princess Regent like everybody else.'

'Let's face it,' Mickey said. 'The only ones who could stop us are the Brigands, and they're currently potty training.'

'Ha!' Nines said. 'Potties are funny because you poo in them.'

The villains began laughing and slapping each other

on the back, congratulating each other for a good day's work. The scarlet mask poked out from Mickey's back pocket as he took a step back from Connie and Nines, right by Lena on the floor.

Charlie's eyebrows shot up. 'Bram,' he whispered. 'The mask.'

'I can't reach it,' she hissed back.

'No, but Lena can.'

Charlie was right.

Lena must have heard, because she shook her head, frustrated. 'What's the point,' she said, as Nines roared with laughter at something Connie said. 'The mask won't work for me.'

Charlie's face lit up. 'It will, it will!' he said excitedly. 'Bram can tell it to work for you.'

'Charlie, be quiet,' Bram shouted.

But it was too late. Mickey spun to face them, a look of pure evil on his face.

Then he pulled the mask from his pocket and sneered. 'Well, well, well. It seems you haven't been entirely honest with me, Bramble.'

CHAPTER
28

'Oh no,' Charlie said. 'I've just made it worse.'

Bram's mind whirred into action and she shouted, 'I can order it to work for my sister, that's all. It only works for family members.'

'It does?' Lena said.

Mickey pulled the scarlet mask back over his head, then pushed the snout of his pistol against Grandpa's temple. 'Order the mask to work for me, or the old man gets it.'

Bram felt light-headed. 'No, please. I'll do anything.' Her voice was ragged at the edges.

'So do it.' He shoved the gun harder into Grandpa's head, causing the old man to wobble in his chair. 'Now.'

'It won't work,' Lena said, desperation climbing in her voice. 'Tell him, Bramble. Tell him it won't work.'

'Then there's no harm in saying it, is there? Surely it's worth a shot.' Mickey laughed at his accidental pun. 'A shot, get it?'

'Good one, boss,' Connie said, as she leant, arms folded, against the cave wall.

Nines shook his head. 'I don't get it.'

'Bramble, don't do it,' Grandpa said, his blue eyes boring into Bram's.

She hovered, torn between wanting to save Grandpa and not wanting Mickey to use the mask for evil. But when she looked at her grandpa's dancing face, it was an easy decision to make.

'I'm sorry,' she whispered, before raising her voice. '*Mask, work for Mickey Ripheart.*'

There was a whoosh, like all the air had been sucked from the cave. The candles flickered and the wind outside began to howl.

Standing in Mickey's place was a man who made other highwaymen look like dolls.

Bram's jaw dropped. She knew that whatever lived

inside the wearer's heart shone through the glamour, but nothing could have prepared her for *this*.

'Well?' Mickey's voice was so deep you could feel it, like the snarl of a bear. 'Am I the Diamond?'

'Oh no, boss,' Connie said, smiling. 'You're much better.'

'And *bigger*,' Nines said, his face full of awe.

The beast before them was a combination of Diamond Jack, Mickey Ripheart and a monster. He was so tall he almost smacked his head against the ceiling, with a back so broad it had split Jack's velvet jacket at the seams. The face was all skull, yet the hair falling around his black eyes was floppy like the ears of a spaniel. When he smiled, he revealed pointy teeth.

Clearly, nothing but hate and violence lived inside Mickey's heart, and right now, it was all Bram could see.

'Cutthroat,' Mickey said. 'I do believe your mask awaits.'

Connie fastened the purple mask around her face.

'I won't do it,' Agnes said.

'Oh, you'll do it.' Mickey repositioned his gun against Grandpa's temple, and Bram noticed that even his gun looked uglier, with a long rusted snout and a warped bone handle.

Agnes took a great, sniffly breath, and whispered, *'Mask, work for Cutthroat Connie.'*

There was a whoosh. A flicker of candles. The howling of the wind.

A strange blend of Connie and Agnes-the-Blade appeared before them. A creature that was taller, spikier, with joints seemingly replaced by blades. A creature that wore Agnes's jacket over the trademark criss-cross of weapon belts, yet had an exaggerated version of Connie's hard face, so that she too looked like a skull. But the most alarming transformation was her hair. She still had her blonde plait, but instead of roping down her back, it writhed in the air behind her as if possessed.

As the creature stood beside monster-Mickey, Bram decided they both looked like a child's drawing, with all of their scariest features exaggerated and made more terrifying.

'Well? How do I look?' Connie asked.

'Like my worst nightmare,' Mickey replied, throwing a sly wink in Lena's direction.

'Have I still got my plait?' she said.

Mickey raised an eyebrow. 'Oh yes. But it's . . . alive.'

Connie nodded, satisfied. 'Oh, we are going to *terrorize* everyone looking like this.'

Bram's heart flipped as she pictured Isabel or Betty and her baby laying eyes on these monsters. Her cheeks grew damp with tears. It just wasn't fair – the magic had always been used for such good, for protecting the one true queen and her loyal subjects, and now it was being twisted.

Mickey passed Nines the blue mask. 'Your turn, Nines.'

'I still want the purple one,' he grumbled, before tying the fabric around his face.

Bram couldn't breathe. Surely Nines couldn't look much worse than he already did.

'OK, One-Shot,' Mickey said. 'You know what to do.'

'*Mask, work for Nines,*' Charlie said, his voice a whimper.

Whoosh. Flicker. Howl.

But for a mop of red hair and a long faded jacket, Nines didn't change.

'Well?' he said in his usual voice.

'Terrifying,' Connie said sarcastically, her braid snaking over her shoulder as if sniffing the air.

'Go on,' Nines said.

'You look the same,' Mickey said. 'But you're ginger.'

Nines patted his head. 'OK. Well, that's good. I like red hair.'

'And you've got ten fingers,' Mickey said.

Nines wiggled his fingers for Connie to see. 'Just call me Ten.'

Agnes managed to sit up, still fighting against her restraints. 'The magic's a glamour. An illusion. Mickey, you aren't actually stronger or bigger. Connie, your plait isn't really a deranged snake, and Nines, your finger is still missing.'

Nines let his hands drop to his sides. 'Spoilsport,' he grumbled.

Mickey narrowed his eyes. 'Image is everything, surely you know that, *Agnes-the-Blade*.' He said her name with a mocking sneer.

'Are we still going to kill Queen Georgina tomorrow?' Nines asked.

'Slight change of plan,' Mickey replied. 'First, we're going to kill the Brigands, and *then* we're going to kill Queen Georgina. And looking like this, it's going to be a piece of cake.'

'Mmm, cake,' Nines mumbled.

Connie's plait whipped from side to side of its own accord. 'I'm not complaining, boss, I love a good slaughter, but I thought the reward money was higher if we delivered the Brigands alive.'

'We can't risk them escaping and reclaiming their masks,' Mickey said, tapping the red material on his face. 'These are worth more than any reward money. Besides, Lavinia will give us everything we could ever want when we kill Queen Georgina.'

Agnes fought against her ropes, a torrent of insults flying from her mouth.

Connie smiled and ran a finger over the handle of her largest blade. 'Good point, boss. Very good point.' She slunk towards Bram, stroking her blade the whole time. 'Can I kill fake-Jack first? That'll teach her to lie.'

Bram felt a scream claw up her throat; dread curdled in her stomach and her chest froze.

'Leave her alone,' Lena yelled.

Mickey raised a hand. 'It's OK, I've got a better idea. Do you remember a while back there was that rats' nest beside the lair?'

Nines shivered. 'Oh, I do, boss. 'Orrible things they were. Used to steal me snacks and chew me boots and nibble me toes when I were asleep.'

'*Was* asleep,' Connie hissed. Her plait took aim as if to strike.

'Shut it,' Nines said.

'And how did we get rid of them?' Mickey asked.

Nines clapped his hands. 'We smoked 'em out, boss. Set a nice little fire at the opening of the nest, we did, so when they ran out we could clobber them over the head.'

'That's right, Nines. And what would have happened had the rats been tied up?' He pointed to the rope around Bram's wrists.

'Dunno, boss.'

Connie chuckled. 'They would have died from smoke inhalation. Wow, Nines, you really don't understand metaphors, do you?'

Nines shook his head.

But Bram did, and it was making her chest so tight she was struggling to breathe.

'So they're the rats,' Mickey said, gesturing to the prisoners. 'And this cave is the nest.' He picked up a candle so it cast spiky shadows up his face, making him look even more horrific. 'And we're going to light another fire. Now do you understand?'

Nines shook his head. 'I thought they was fish.'

'We're going to smoke them to death, you idiot,' Connie said. 'Now grab the sack of weapons and let's go burn things.'

Nines hoisted the sack over his shoulder and headed towards the exit.

'No,' Bram whispered, 'no, no, no.'

She heard the soft sobs of Charlie, the groaning of her sister, and Agnes's desperate wails as she continued to strain against her ropes. Yet everything was distant and far away, like she was listening through water. She slumped on her bottom unable to shake the feeling that this was all her fault.

If only she hadn't gone into the shed.

If only she hadn't found the mask.

'Bye, Brigands,' Mickey said. 'We've got a date with Queen Georgina.'

'Stand and deliver,' Connie said, twizzling a knife around her fingers. 'Your money or your life.'

'More like, your *magic* or your life,' Mickey said.

And with that, the terrifying trio swept from the cave.

CHAPTER
29

Through a film of shock, Bram listened to the sound of branches being stacked at the mouth of the cave. *We're going to die.* The thought was a spear, puncturing her heart and releasing a flood of terror into her veins. Agnes and Grandpa struggled against their bindings, whilst Lena began chewing at the ropes around her wrists.

Charlie was crying softly, his knees curled up to his head. 'It's all my fault,' he whispered. 'It's all my fault.'

Bram leant against him. 'No, it's not. It's my fault.' A heavy boot of shame slammed into her body; the air rushed from her lungs and she sobbed. 'I should never have gone into the shed. I should never have answered the mask's calls.'

'I did tell you,' Lena said, before returning to gnaw at her fastenings.

'Lena,' Grandpa said. 'That's enough.'

The Rippers' laughter floated into the chamber, followed by the rattle of a tinderbox and the faint scent of smoke. Bram was transported back to the emporium, back to their neat little kitchen, where Grandpa used to shake their very own tinderbox and say, 'Let's get warm, Bramble.' She wanted to go home so badly her entire body thrummed with longing.

Soon, the Rippers left, taking their laughter and jeers with them. Long, grey fingers of smoke began reaching into the cave, carrying the hiss of flames – and the sound of a dog barking. Bram didn't pay much attention to the dog, she was too busy crying and coughing to think about the animals outside. Then she realized that it wasn't just any dog. It was . . .

'Bertie?' she said.

A familiar voice broke through their stone prison: 'Well done, Bertie-boos. Good doggy.'

Bram's heart doubled in size, brimming with hope,

relief, happiness.

She released a tear-sodden laugh. 'It's Ernest. Every-one, Ernest's here!'

The prisoners all cried out, 'Ernest! Ernest! Help! We're in here.' The friends began thumping their feet against the floor, and Grandpa toppled his chair in a bid to be heard.

'Hang on,' Ernest called. 'I'm coming.'

The sound of stamping and cursing was followed by the swish of branches dragging across stone. Bram imagined her best friend stomping out flames and hurling smouldering boughs from his path and was overwhelmed with pride.

Footsteps echoed around the passageway and Ernest burst into the smoky chamber like a ray of light. He wore a pink highwayman mask that he'd clearly cut from Lena's best gown, and carried the knife the Brigands used for skinning rabbits – a knife perfect for slicing through ropes.

He beamed. 'Don't tell me I'm the only one with a mask now?'

'Ernest!' Bram said, her voice shaking with joy. 'How did you find us?'

Bertie circled his feet, yapping, sending the candles

flickering and the smoke swirling, and Bram understood immediately that the terrier had led him here.

'Bertie was very insistent,' Ernest said, rushing to help with her binds. 'I think he woke up the entire Forest of Bells with all his barking.'

'Good Bertie-boos,' Bram said, half laughing, half crying with relief. 'Good doggy.'

The next few minutes were a haze of rope-cutting, smiling faces and embraces, followed by a dash towards the smoke-free air of the Crooked Woods. For a moment, Bram stood with her friends beneath the night sky, coughing the smoke from her lungs and gazing at the stars – never before had she been so grateful to inhale the scent of earth and moss.

She turned to Grandpa and pulled him into a hug. 'Grandpa! Are you OK? I've been so worried.'

'Just a bit sore from being tied up,' he said, flexing his hands and massaging his wrists. 'And I could murder a cuppa and a cookie.'

Lena pointed to Ernest's face. 'Seriously? You hacked up my best gown?'

'Sorry, I just wanted to feel the part,' he said, sheepish.

She shrugged. 'I never liked that dress much

anyway. Apparently the fabric isn't even real silk.'

'So what happened here?' Ernest asked. 'Where are your masks?'

'We'll explain on the way,' Agnes said, gesturing towards the shelter of the trees. 'We've got a queen to save.'

CHAPTER

30

By the time they'd reached the glen and tended to the horses, dawn was fast approaching. Rubbing their tired eyes, they headed back to the hideaway, where Charlie handed out leather pouches of water and chipped bowls filled with berries. The friends huddled beneath frayed blankets.

'OK, Grandpa,' Lena said from her perch on a rickety chair. 'You need to tell us everything that happened while you were held hostage. Any little detail could help.' She was still wearing her camouflage gear; Bram had initially mistaken the dark circles beneath her eyes for patches of mud.

Grandpa, who was sitting on the floor beside Bram, glanced up from his snack – he was on his third bowl, which was understandable considering he hadn't eaten in days. 'What do you want to know?'

'Did you see their lair?' Charlie asked. He was resting on the floor cushions beside Agnes, with Bertie snoozing on his lap.

'Did they talk about their plan to hold up Queen Georgina?' Agnes asked.

Grandpa sipped his water, a thoughtful expression playing across his features. 'I was in their lair to begin with, I think. They kept me blindfolded so I couldn't see anything.'

Lena sighed with frustration. 'So you didn't learn anything?'

'I didn't say that,' he replied. 'I learnt that the cave is close to the lair, so their hideout is definitely in the Crooked Woods just as we've always suspected, and' – he paused to tap his ears – 'I heard everything they said. I suppose they were planning to kill me, so they grew careless.'

Bram tried not to think about how close she'd come to losing Grandpa. She laid a hand on his arm, savouring the softness of his blanket as it sank against his spindly arms.

Agnes leant forward. 'So? What did you hear?'

'Well, I know exactly when and where they intend to hold up Queen Georgina's carriage,' Grandpa said.

'OK,' Agnes said, falling back with relief. 'OK. So we can intervene and stop the kidnapping, and once the one true queen reclaims her throne, she can send Lavinia to prison. We just need to get Georgina from the hospital to the palace safely.' A wistful look crossed her face. 'Then everything can go back to how it used to be.'

A silence passed between them as they considered the great task at hand. Bram stared at the remaining weapons: a few knives, a couple of rusted guns, a catapult.

'We're never going to protect the Queen with that lot,' Charlie said as if reading her mind. He'd freed his red curls from the prison of his hat, but the stripes of dirt still remained on his cheeks and chin. 'Nines has got my lucky gun.'

'And Connie's got my weapon belts,' Agnes said.

'He took my stuff too,' Lena said.

Grandpa popped another berry in his mouth.

'We've got everything we need, don't you worry.'

'Bagsy the catapult,' Ernest said. 'I once shot Mr Wren right on the bum and he never even knew it was me.'

Lena's features pinched together. 'There's absolutely zero chance you're tagging along, Ernest.'

'What?' he said, leaping to his feet. 'You can't be serious. I literally just rescued you from the Rippers.'

Bertie began to bark.

'Technically, Bertie rescued us,' Lena replied.

'It was a joint effort,' Ernest said. 'Bram, tell her I can come.'

Lena scoffed. 'She's not coming either. It's far too dangerous.'

'That's not fair,' Bram said, and upon speaking the words, she realized that the fear she'd felt back at the hold-ups was slowly ebbing away. She didn't feel ready to be a highwayman, not yet, but neither did she want to be cast to the side. Perhaps she wouldn't order the mask to work for Lena after all. 'The mask chose me for a reason,' she said.

'Yes, because it didn't realize how utterly useless you'd be,' Lena snapped.

Bram gasped.

'Lena,' Grandpa warned.

'You take that back,' Ernest said.

Agnes was shaking her head, looking more distressed by the minute. 'But Bram has to come. We may get the masks back – she can order the red mask to work for you, Lena.'

'No,' Ernest said. 'Lena doesn't get to be Jack any more, the mask chose Bram. Bram can hold her own!'

'This is for the Queen,' Agnes said. '*The one true queen*. We need to put up a fight and Lena's the best Jack there ever was.'

'Debatable,' Grandpa said.

Lena folded her arms and blew a curl of hair from her eyes. 'Fine. Bram can go. But only if she lets me be Diamond Jack when we get the masks. And no waving sticks around and nearly getting shot like a fool.'

Charlie stood. 'Stop being so mean, Lena. You don't get to be the boss any more – you abandoned us.'

'Can we please focus on how to save Queen Georgina,' Agnes said, hands holding her head as if trying to stop herself from falling apart.

'Yeah, Lena.' Ernest stuck out his tongue and Bertie barked even louder.

'Oh, you're such a baby.' Lena stood and began wagging her finger.

'Couldn't-be-meaner-Jaquelena,' Ernest sang, at the same time Agnes said, 'Don't any of you care about the Queen?'

It wasn't long before everyone was on their feet, shouting and pointing, faces scrunched with hurt and anger – everyone except Grandpa, who was still eating his berries.

An image of the Rippers elbowed into Bram's mind. Connie was threatening to chop off another of Nines's fingers, Nines was attempting to strangle her, and Mickey stood by, telling them off for behaving like children while secretly enjoying the fact they both were under his control.

'We're behaving like *them*,' she whispered to herself. Then louder, she yelled, 'STOP!'

The voices dropped, Bertie stopped yapping, and everyone looked at her.

'Bram? What is it?' Ernest asked.

'We're behaving like the Rippers,' Bram said. 'Bickering and name-calling. And we're better than that. We're better than *them*. Instead of tearing each other down, we should be raising each other up.'

Charlie inhaled sharply. 'Oh my goodness, you're right.'

The others nodded, sheepish, while Lena blushed and said, 'Sorry, sis.'

'Come on,' Bram said, looking at each of them in turn. 'Let's focus on our strengths.' She turned to Charlie and smiled. 'Charlie, you're the best shot in the queendom and you're only eleven. *Eleven*. You don't need a lucky gun because luck has nothing to do with it. You're pure talent.'

A shy smile crossed Charlie's lips and he picked up the rusty gun, weighing it in his hands.

'And Agnes,' Bram said. 'You don't need those belts. I mean, they look scary, but you could take down an army with an old kitchen knife.'

'Before breakfast,' Agnes said, pretending to hurl a blade.

Bram looked at her sister. 'Lena, I've seen you catch a fish with your bare hands, and you saved me from that coachman when I didn't even notice him pull a weapon. You're quick and clever and' – she laughed – 'maybe just a bit bossy. But we can use that. When we come up with a plan, I know you'll make sure we all stick to our parts.'

Lena smiled. 'Thanks, Bramble.'

'Do me, do me,' Ernest said, pressing his hands

together in a pleading motion.

'Ernest,' Bram said, her voice welling with affection. 'Maybe rescuing us was a joint effort with Bertie, but the only reason we have Bertie is because *you* saved him from the turnspit. You made us the best camouflage clothes we could have asked for, and nobody knows as much about highwaymen as you. We can use that to our advantage.'

'Yes, yes, yes,' he said, jiggling between his feet. 'I've read every newspaper clipping and heard every bit of gossip – I can tell you anything you need to know about the Rippers. Like did you know Nines is worried that Connie and Mickey are going to run away together and chuck him out of the group? And Connie thinks Mickey doesn't take her as seriously because he thinks women aren't strong. And word is, Mickey has his sights on the throne.' He squealed with excitement.

'And Grandpa,' Bram said, turning to her grand-father with a smile. 'I know that you used to be Diamond Jack and you can fight and shoot and throw knives, but what amazes me is how nothing ever rattles you. You'll keep us calm and together. I know it.'

'Thanks, dear heart,' he said, chewing on a berry.

Encouraged by their smiling faces, Bram continued.

'Maybe the Rippers have got our magic masks, but we've got something they haven't got.'

'Personal hygiene?' Ernest said.

'Yes,' Bram said, with a giggle. 'But also, we're a team.'

'Yeah,' Charlie shouted.

'We're so much stronger when we're together. We're like, we're like . . .' She scrabbled about for an example, before falling upon a familiar memory. Her stomach squeezed and her chest grew tight. But instead of pushing the memory away, she let it fill her head – the blur of vivid colours, the smell of popcorn, the sound of laughter and applause, the beat of the drum roll.

She took a deep breath. 'We're like the circus.'

'What?' Charlie and Agnes said.

'My parents took Lena and me to the circus the night before they died. It's not something I think about much because it hurts so much to remember how happy we were.' Her voice cracked and Lena rushed to her, arms outstretched.

'Oh, Bramble,' she said, pulling her into a quick hug.

Using her sister's comfort, Bram steadied her voice. 'So there were all these individual acts. Clowns, acrobats, jugglers, men being shot from cannons. And they were great, really great, but the best bit was at the end when they all came together for the finale. It was' – she faltered – 'it was mind-blowing.'

'I remember,' Lena said, her eyes glazing. 'The ring was filled with movement and action and they all worked together to create the perfect ending.'

'Well, that's like us,' Bram said. 'That's how we'll win. By sticking together and working as a team.'

'That's really nice, Bramble,' Lena said. 'So how are we going to save Queen Georgina from the Rippers?'

'I've got a plan,' Bram said.

CHAPTER
31

As Bram left the safety of the Forest of Bells, the sun burst over the horizon, painting the moorland in oranges and pinks; she was dazzled by the beauty of it all and let the constant beat of Dusty's hooves chase any fear from her body. Ernest sat behind her, one arm curled around her middle and the other holding Bertie to his chest. Their friends cantered alongside them.

From behind her, Ernest pointed towards the royal hospital high on Rosemary Hill. 'There, that's where Queen Georgina's coming from.'

To reach the palace, the Queen had to travel north to south, crossing the vast moorland that separated the Forest of Bells in the west from the Crooked Woods in the east. And it was there, whilst exposed on the moor, that the Rippers planned to steal the Queen.

They paused at a line of trees. Grandpa, who was sitting behind Lena atop the piebald horse, dismounted and peered through the branches.

'That's where they plan to stop the royal carriage.' He pointed to a dirt path in the distance. 'Do you see? The track leading from Rosemary Hill to the city? Well, there's a point where the moorland begins to slope upwards.'

'It'll slow the royal convoy down,' Bram said, looking at the hill and recalling her first hold-up.

'Very good, Bramble,' he replied. 'Carriages don't fare so well uphill.'

Agnes's face creased with anxiety. 'So the Rippers are just going to attack out in the open? No trees to jump out from, no rocks to hide behind?'

'That's what they said,' Grandpa replied.

Lena looked thoughtful for a moment. 'But if the Rippers are coming from the Crooked Woods, won't the guards see them coming? Won't Queen Georgina have time to escape?'

'It's so she can't run and hide in the trees,' Agnes said, her voice pulled between bitterness and sorrow.

They all turned to look at her.

'What do you mean?' Bram asked.

Agnes blinked back a tear. 'If Georgina manages to slip away during the commotion, then where's she going to go? There's no hiding on a moor.'

Bram tried not to think of poor Queen Georgina fleeing the hold-up, sprinting as fast as she could across the open plain, only to be spotted and chased down by monster-Mickey on horseback.

After a pause, Bram said, 'So how long have we got until they arrive?'

'Not long,' Grandpa replied. 'They're transporting Queen Georgina soon after dawn whilst the roads are clear. The journey's supposed to be a secret.'

Bram didn't know how long they waited, their hearts hammering, yet the sun had barely climbed in the sky when she caught her first glimpse of the royal convoy – a shimmering snake descending Rosemary Hill.

'There,' Ernest said. 'There's the one true queen.'

'Just remind me why we didn't go to the hospital to warn her?' Charlie said.

Lena rolled her eyes. 'We've been over this. Princess Lavinia will realize we're on to her and they'll just delay the journey to another time.'

'A time we won't know about,' Grandpa said. 'Because I won't be there eavesdropping.'

'Besides,' Lena said, 'if we catch the Rippers in the act, they'll be charged with high treason.'

Bram focused on the snake in the distance, growing larger and clearer as it reached the moor. The sound of hooves against grass and the rumble of the carriage wheels echoed in the breeze. Bram picked out two carriages, one gold, one silver, flanked by a line of guards; she guessed immediately that the one true queen was in the golden one and the Princess Regent was in the silver.

'Why aren't the Queen and Lavinia sharing a carriage?' Bram asked.

'It's customary for the royal family to travel in different carriages,' Agnes said. 'There's more chance of one of them surviving in an attack.' She shook her head, her face fixed in a scowl. 'Lavinia's so crafty. She's only here so people don't accuse her of being involved in the kidnapping – she can't be involved if she's attacked too.'

The convoy grew closer and closer. Soon, the Rippers would emerge from the Crooked Woods, and then she and her friends would try to defend the Queen and deliver her safely to the palace. All without their masks. The self-doubt made her limbs weak.

'Does everyone remember the plan?' Lena said.

They all nodded, except for Agnes, who, in an unusually fragile voice, said, 'What if it doesn't work?'

'It'll be OK, Aggy,' Lena said. 'We'll save her, don't worry.'

'Thanks,' Agnes said with a sniff.

Lena tilted her head. 'Wait, aren't you going to tell me to call you Agnes?'

Agnes smiled. 'It's OK. You can call me Aggy now.'

'And you can call me Chuck,' Charlie said.

'We understand why you left,' Agnes said, eyes fixed on the golden carriage. 'I'd do anything to protect my sister too.'

'Thanks, guys,' Lena said, blinking quickly and mumbling something about dirt getting in her eyes.

She gave up being Jack for me, Bram thought with a wave of love. She finally understood just what a sacrifice it must have been. Not only did her sister give up the thrill and the adventure, the joy of helping the villagers, but she left her best friends, just so she could be there for Bram.

Bram reached across and squeezed Lena's arm. 'Thank you,' she whispered.

An unreadable expression touched her sister's features, then her lips set in a resolute line. 'Look, Bramble. If you get the mask back, you keep it. Don't order it to work for me.'

'What?' Bram said.

'Charlie's right.' She smiled a sad yet accepting smile. '*You're* Diamond Jack now. The mask chose you, and I'm just going to have to accept that.' She reached over and gently pulled Bram's locket out from under her apron. 'When Mama and Papa died, I gave up the mask so I could spend more time with you, so I could watch you and make sure you were safe. I just couldn't bear the thought of losing you too.'

'I know, Lena,' Bram said. 'I understand—'

'No.' Lena cut over her. 'You don't.' She lowered her eyes. 'The thing is, I wanted to stay safe too. Mama and Papa's deaths scared me. If they could die in a freak accident, no villains, no weapons, no masks, just a terrible accident, well then . . .' She tailed off. 'The world stopped being safe.'

Nobody spoke. The breeze shook the leaves and an arrow of birds flew overhead. Lena had always seemed so self-assured, so confident. Was she just as scared as Bram beneath the surface?

Lena took a shaky breath and patted the piebald's neck. 'But the thing is, Bramble, if you hide from the world, you miss out on so much. And I don't want you to miss out any more. The mask is yours now.'

Grandpa rested his head on Lena's shoulder. 'Well done, Jaquelena. I couldn't be more proud of you.'

She nodded and sniffed back her tears.

'Lena, I—' Bram wanted to say thank you, but the only words that formed on her tongue were filled with uncertainty. *What if I'm not ready to be Diamond Jack? What if I'm not good enough? Not brave enough?* 'But I can't throw a knife or shoot a gun,' she eventually said. 'I'm not really a highwayman.'

'That's not what the magic masks are about,' she replied. 'Not really.'

'They're about being pure of heart,' Charlie said, covering his heart with his hand.

'And protecting the one true queen,' Agnes said, copying his gesture.

Grandpa smiled from behind Lena. 'You'll make a

fantastic Jack, Bramble.'

Bram could feel Ernest fidgeting behind her. He pulled the toy pistol from his belt. 'It looks like you'll be needing this after all.' He waggled his eyebrows as she turned to take it.

'Thank you,' she said, laughing as she tucked it into the waistband of her apron. It wouldn't do much good, but she knew Ernest meant well.

'I'm sorry if I've been too hard on you,' Lena said, her voice so low only Bram and Ernest could hear. 'Do you forgive me?'

'Oh, Lena,' Bram began, but her throat tightened and she found she couldn't speak.

Ernest saved her, swinging open his arms. 'Bring it in for a hug, couldn't-be-meaner-Jaquelena.'

Laughing, Lena leant from her horse and wrapped her arms around Bram and Ernest.

'When we're back at the hideaway, I'll start teaching you how to aim. Deal?' Lena said.

The idea of Lena giving her shooting lessons filled Bram with a surprising joy. Yes, it would give Lena an opportunity to boss her around again, but after everything that had happened, she didn't mind so much.

'Deal,' she replied, smiling.

'Sorry to break up the moment, but they're getting near,' Agnes said, pointing through the branches.

While they'd been reconciling, the convoy had almost reached the slope.

'Any minute now . . .' Lena said, standing up in her stirrups so she could get a better look.

'Look,' Agnes said, glancing at Bram and Ernest, her voice apprehensive. 'Before things kick off, there's something I need to tell you.'

Yet Bram was only half listening. She was too intent on watching the vast treeline of the Crooked Woods. Where were the Rippers?

'Grandpa,' Bram said. 'What exactly did the Rippers say about holding up Queen Georgina's carriage?'

'They said they'd wait till she reached the grassy knoll on the moor so the carriage couldn't outrun them, then they'd appear.'

'Appear from where?' she asked.

'The Crooked Woods,' Grandpa said with a shrug.

'Did they say that?' she asked, still scanning the twisted trees.

'Oh dear,' he said as he stroked his beard. 'Now that you mention it, I'm not sure they did.'

'Everyone, please,' Agnes said. 'I need to tell Bram and Ernest something.'

But everyone's attention was fixed on the royal convoy: two gilded carriages, each with a fancy coach-man and four white horses, a line of mounted guards leading the way and bringing up the rear. There wasn't anything unusual.

Wait. Bram did a double take. Something wasn't right about the three guards at the back of the convoy. Scrunching her face, she tried to get a better look. It was their uniforms. They didn't sparkle as brightly in the new morning sun.

'Ernest,' she whispered. 'Those guards at the back of the line . . .'

'Imitation silk,' Ernest gushed. 'Cheap rip-off fabric. Those uniforms are fake.'

'Hurry,' Bram said, panic exploding through her body as she urged Dusty through the trees and broke cover.

'Bram, get back here,' Lena shouted.

Just before Bram squeezed Dusty's middle and began sailing across the moor, she shouted, 'Every-body, follow me. The Rippers are part of the convoy. They're dressed as guards.'

CHAPTER

32

Thundering across the moor, the wind in her hair and the drum of the hooves in her heart, Bram saw the fake guards pull brightly coloured strips of fabric from their breeches. *The magic masks*, she thought. With horror, she watched as the Rippers pulled them over their heads and transformed into their monstrous counterparts, the fake uniforms no longer visible beneath the glamour.

Bram urged Dusty on and Ernest tightened his grip around her waist. She could only pray he didn't drop poor Bertie.

Mickey finally turned to see them. A smile crossed his angular face and his teeth shone like blades in the morning sun. He didn't look in the slightest bit afraid; Bram had never felt more like a kid.

'Quickly,' Mickey roared, his voice a rumble across the moor.

The Rippers overtook the guards and circled to the front of the convoy.

Connie's plait swished through the air as she drew two blades, and Nines pulled two pistols from his belt.

'Stand and deliver,' Mickey roared.

Upon seeing the horrific highwaymen half of the guards fled, their spooked horses galloping into the Crooked Woods. Only ten or so loyal guards remained, raising their weapons and spinning their heads frantically between the approaching Brigands and the monsters on horseback, trying to assess who was the greatest risk to Queen Georgina.

We're nearly there. You can do this, Bram told herself. *You can do this.*

She glanced at her fearless family and friends. Agnes and Lena gripped the reins of their horses with one hand and raised knives in the other, whereas Charlie and Grandpa drew their pistols. They released a battle cry, and with a quiver of shame, Bram pulled on her reins, bringing Dusty to a trot so she could fall behind the others. Whilst nobody was looking, she looped round the back of Queen Georgina's carriage and slipped from sight.

Thick red curtains hung from the carriage windows, blocking the passengers from view. Bram tried not to picture the Queen inside, terrified and confused. As quietly as possible, Bram and Ernest dropped from Dusty and crawled beneath the royal carriage. The dew-sodden grass soaked through Bram's clothes, but they could see the battle in action.

Adrenalin flooded Bram's body as she heard gunshots, the cries of rage, and saw the glint of flying knives. Boots passed so close to the carriage she could see the spots of blood dappling the leather, and when the odd guard hit the ground, clutching at an injury, she bit back her screams. She thought of her darling grandpa, her sister and her new friends caught up in the fighting. *Please be OK, please be OK*. It felt so wrong, quivering under a carriage while her friends and family went to war.

Ernest lay beside her, sweat trickling down his face. They touched little fingers. He was still wearing his pink highwayman mask, and Bertie, who trembled beside them, was dressed in a matching pink dog-coat. If Bram hadn't been so frightened, she would have loved the cuteness.

'It's nearly over,' Ernest whispered.

The battle sounds began to fade. Weapons were thrown to the ground. Cries of surrender and the jeers of the Rippers replaced the clash of swords and the pop of bullets.

Her ears ringing with anxiety, her heart thudding so hard she was worried it might burst from her chest, Bram squinted across the grass: kneeling not far from them were Lena, Grandpa, Agnes, Charlie and a few guards, all unarmed and subdued, and to Bram's relief, uninjured. And dancing around them were the Rippers, throwing victorious gunfire and whoops of joy into the morning air.

The villains had won.

CHAPTER
33

Her breath began to quicken, the panic rising like floodwater.

'It's OK,' Ernest whispered. 'This is all part of the plan, remember?'

Bram nodded; she had to remain calm. Plotting it back at the treehouse and seeing it play out in real life, however, were two very different things.

Bertie whimpered and Ernest stroked his muzzle. 'Hush, boy,' he said.

'Shall we kill 'em now?' It was Nines's voice.

The sound of a carriage door clicking open caused

Bram to freeze. But it wasn't near enough to be the Queen's door, and Bram quickly realized it was a door of the silver carriage swinging open. A voice rang out – female and strangely familiar. 'Not yet, Nines. I would like to see who dares interfere with my plan.'

Two silver shoes strode across the grass towards Bram's friends. Bram could just make out the back of a silver gown and the back of an elaborate white wig.

The Princess Regent.

Bowing, Mickey gestured towards the prisoners. 'Princess Lavinia, may I present to you the terrifying Brigands.'

Connie and Nines cackled with glee.

'They're just dumb kids,' Nines said.

'And an old man,' Connie said.

But Lavinia didn't laugh. Instead, she said in a thin voice, 'Beatrice? Is it really you?'

Bram could just pick out Agnes's features, filled with defiance and hatred as she glared towards Lavinia. 'Yes,' Agnes said, her voice stiff. 'Yes, *darling* sister. It's me. Beatrice. The missing princess.'

CHAPTER 34

The shock momentarily pushed aside any fear, and Bram cast her mind back over the past few days. Everything slotted neatly into place. Agnes's reluctance to talk about her background, her sheer determination to rescue Queen Georgina. It was because Agnes was the missing princess. And when she'd told Bram about her own sister, the one who was so envious and thought of her as a threat, she was talking about Lavinia.

But masks always ran in families, didn't they? Bram's mind worked quickly. Perhaps because Agnes was royalty, because she was related to the queen who enchanted the masks all those years ago, the mask still recognized her.

'So that's what Agnes was trying to tell us before we stormed the hold-up,' Bram whispered to Ernest.

He shook his head in disbelief. 'I didn't recognize her out of the royal garb! Oh no.' He froze. 'She's seen me pick my nose.' He flushed. 'I've *farted* in front of her.'

Dumbfounded, they turned their attention back to the drama unfolding on the moor.

'So you're a Brigand now?' Lavinia said, laughing. 'You always were Georgie's little pet.'

'Protector, not pet,' Agnes snarled.

'Then I was right to get rid of you,' Lavinia said. 'You were always sticking your nose in my business – Georgie's little spy. And then you'd whip her up against me. Why, if I hadn't got rid of you, Georgina would have got rid of *me*.'

'That's where you're wrong,' Agnes said. 'Georgie would never have got rid of you. She's not like you, Lavinia. She's good – she cares about you.'

Lavinia raised an eyebrow. 'Dare I ask how you ended up holding up rich folk instead of feeding the fishes? Last time I saw you, you were tied up in the back of a carriage about to be dropped in the ocean.'

Agnes's face could barely hold all her rage. 'I'm alive because One-Shot Charlie and Diamond Jack held up my carriage. They saved me.'

Charlie piped up. 'We were hoping for treasure. And we found it.'

Lena nodded. 'The third member of the Brigands, Bertha, had just retired, and she didn't have anyone to pass the purple mask on to, so we had an extra mask. And when we held up Agnes's carriage, that mask glowed hot in my pocket.'

'You could say the mask chose her,' Charlie said with a smile.

Lavinia chuckled, the back of her dress trembling. 'Oh, I've never heard anything more ridiculous. Three children are the Brigands. My *little sister*, a Brigand. Well, thank goodness *we* have the magic masks now.' She gestured to the terrifying highwaymen surrounding them. 'I must confess, when Mickey Ripheart told me about the magic masks, I had no idea they'd be quite so ... effective.'

'You haven't got a mask,' Charlie said, his face innocent. 'Have you?'

'What do you mean?' Lavinia snapped.

Charlie shrugged. 'You said *we*, when really, the Rippers have the magic masks. Not you. Though I'm sure they'll let you have them if you want them.'

Lavinia's voice flickered with uncertainty. 'Well, of course they will.'

Grandpa spoke up next. 'I see you've still got all ten fingers, Nines.'

'That's your cue,' Ernest nudged Bram. 'Go get the Queen.'

Bram nodded, but her body refused to move. 'I don't know if I can do this,' she managed to croak.

Ernest grinned. 'Of course you can. You're Bramble Browning. You can do anything. And I'm right here, cheering you on. We all are.'

Instinctively, Bram's fingers landed on her silver locket. Ernest was right. He was right there, as were Grandpa, Lena, Charlie and Agnes. But also, her parents. Not in flesh, but their memory, their strength and love, it was still with her. Always. She turned the locket in her fingers, and for the first time since her parents' death, she clicked it open. Her parents' portraits smiled out at her. Oh, how she'd missed their lovely faces. She felt the familiar sorrow, of course she did, but she also felt an enormous sense of happiness and comfort.

'Thanks, Ernest,' she whispered, and instead of tucking the locket back beneath her clothes, she let it glint, unhidden, from her neck.

Then, taking a deep breath, she dropped a kiss on Bertie's head and whispered, 'Good luck, boy,' before slipping from beneath the carriage on the opposite side to the drama.

Pausing for a moment, checking she was alone and unnoticed, she listened closely to the Brigands pick at the existing cracks in the Rippers' relationships, just as they'd planned back at the treehouse.

'How did you lose your finger, Nines?' Lena asked.

'Cutthroat did it,' Nines replied.

Next, Grandpa spoke. 'I bet Mickey was cross with her when she did that.'

'I think he just laughed, didn't you, boss?' Nines said.

Mickey growled.

Slowly, Bram gripped the handle of the carriage door. The curtains still blocked her view inside. She hoped Queen Georgina was waiting and not some trickster guard ready to blast her away. Steadying her breath, she began inching open the door.

Charlie's voice sailed towards her. 'I suppose Mickey would take Connie's side, considering they're planning to run away together.'

'What?' Lavinia said.

'I knew it,' Nines shouted.

The door opened fully to reveal a terrified young woman, huddled alone on a velvet seat. She wore no crown, but her dress was a pale gold and lavishly embroidered. She looked like an older version of Agnes, with dark brown skin, large fawn eyes and black hair looped around her head.

Pressing a finger to her lips, Bram clambered inside the carriage and gently shut the door. 'Come with me, Your Majesty,' she whispered.

'Who are you?' Queen Georgina asked, her voice trembling.

'Beatrice sent me.'

Her face creased with confusion. 'Beatrice? My little Bea? But she's dead.'

Bram realized she could no longer make out the chatter from outside. The carriage was mostly soundproof. Poor Queen Georgina must have been petrified, not knowing what was happening outside, with just the muffled sound of gunshot and the odd battle cry.

Bram smiled. 'Oh, I promise you, Bea's very much alive. Quickly, now.'

The Queen decided Bram was indeed her best option. She allowed herself to be helped from the carriage door so they both stood in the open air, pressing themselves against the gilded side so they were out of view.

Grandpa's voice reached them. 'I overheard loads of conversations while I was in the lair. Mickey thinks Connie is a rubbish highwayman because she's a woman.'

'What?' Connie said, her voice pitching with rage.

'I never said that,' Mickey said.

Bram coaxed Dusty towards her and patted her nose. 'Wait for it,' she whispered at Queen Georgina.

The sound of Lena sighing filled the air. 'I guess it makes sense for Mickey to marry Connie. He'll need a queen when he overthrows Lavinia.'

Lavinia raised her voice. 'Planning to overthrow me, are you, Mickey?'

As the arguing continued, the cracks in the Rippers' relationships grew wider and wider, the lack of trust tearing them apart. Bram ducked down and tugged on

Ernest's trouser leg.

'Now,' she mouthed to him.

Ernest set the terrier on the floor and checked his underbelly, running his fingers beneath the pink coat and the secret compartment he'd stitched there. The secret compartment that contained a dainty pistol.

'Go to Charlie,' Ernest whispered into his fuzzy ear.

Bertie trotted off in the direction of the Rippers.

The plan's working, Bram thought. *It's really working.* By allowing themselves to get caught, the Brigands had created enough of a distraction for Bram to secure Queen Georgina, and any moment now, Bertie would deliver the hidden pistol to Charlie.

Bram almost couldn't believe how smoothly it was all going. Bubbling with joy, she mounted Dusty and pulled the Queen up behind her.

Three shots rang through the air.

She angled Dusty so she could see around the carriage.

Charlie held the dainty pistol and a happy Bertie danced around his feet. Connie's knife had been blasted from her hand, Nines's pistol lay mangled on the ground, and Lavinia's wig had been shot from her head revealing the thick, black curls beneath. Bram couldn't stop grinning as Agnes reclaimed her weapons belt from Connie and lifted the mask from her face. Connie's blonde plait fell lifeless against her back, and she shrank back to her regular size. Then Grandpa and Lena barrelled into Nines, bringing him to the floor with a thud, and Charlie took back his blue mask, transforming the highwayman back into plain old Nines.

And Mickey . . .

Wait. Where was Mickey?

Her eyes searched frantically while her heart flipped in her chest.

She squeezed Dusty's sides, ready to flee, when she heard the click of a pistol.

Mickey stood beside them, gun aimed straight at the Queen.

'Going somewhere?' he growled.

CHAPTER 35

Mickey still wore Bram's red mask, and when he grinned, his teeth were a row of barbs.

'Did you honestly think I wouldn't notice your pathetic distraction?' he said.

Before Bram could urge Dusty onwards, Mickey lunged towards her and grabbed a handful of her smock. She kicked out, swung her fists, but the thug was simply too strong. He plucked her from the saddle and dumped her on the ground as if she were a doll.

'Stop,' she gasped, stumbling to her feet, desperately reaching for Queen Georgina.

But Mickey was already sitting behind the monarch, stretching around her with his tree-trunk arms so he could grip the reins. Her dress frothed round Dusty's neck, the pale gold material blending into the horse's palomino coat, and she reached a slender hand towards Bram, her pretty face caught between terror and acceptance.

Bram made a final grab, and for a brief moment their fingers connected, then Mickey booted Dusty and they shot away.

'No!' Bram screamed.

They didn't get far.

Bram could only assume that after hearing her master's voice, Dusty decided she'd had enough of the bully on her back. She dug her hooves into the ground, skidded to a halt and dipped her head so her neck became a yellow slide.

Good girl, Bram thought.

Queen Georgina slid to the ground and landed in a heap.

Bram began to run just as Georgina leapt to her feet.

'Your Majesty, quickly,' Bram shouted.

The Queen hoisted up her skirts and started to

sprint from her captor, but one of her heels sank into the mud, whilst the other caught in her petticoats. And Mickey wasn't about to give up. Jumping from Dusty's back, he stampeded after the Queen. Before Bram could make any progress, he'd scooped up Georgina and thrown her over his shoulder like a sack of turnips.

He pelted towards the Crooked Woods, the Queen screaming and wriggling. If he made it to the trees, it wouldn't matter that he was on foot. The forest would slow the horses and he'd simply disappear amongst the gnarly branches and low-hanging mist.

'Oh no you don't,' Bram whispered.

As if sensing her plan, Dusty appeared at her side.

'Good girl,' Bram said, mounting so smoothly that in any other circumstance, she would have paused to celebrate. But there was no time. So instead, she touched her locket and let the memory of her parents fill her mind, then she squeezed Dusty with her feet.

'Come on, girl,' she shouted.

Dusty launched into action. Bram let the drum roll of hooves wash over her. She closed her eyes for a moment, and for the first time since they had gone, she was able to see her parents' smiling faces as they rode beside her through the countryside.

Mickey was fast approaching the darkness of the Crooked Woods. The shadows stretched towards him. But Dusty was a whir of hooves and determination.

Only when level with his huge lumping back did Bram remember she had no weapons, no fighting skills, so she acted on pure instinct, balancing on Dusty's back in a wobbly crouching position and drawing on the only advantage she had: momentum. Propelling herself to the side, she leapt from Dusty's back and bowled through the air like a human cannon. Like a trapeze artist.

She landed square on top of Mickey and Queen Georgina with a loud *doof*.

Mickey's legs gave way. He collapsed like an over-loaded table, sending the trio tumbling to the ground in a mess of limbs and flying earth. Pain wrapped around Bram's chest as she thudded against the grass.

In the distance, she heard the cry of her friends and family: *Bram, be careful. We're coming.*

Her head woozy from the fall, she managed to clasp a handful of golden fabric and pulled Georgina from the mud.

'Hurry, Your Majesty,' she garbled, as they both

began to stumble away from the trees.

The drum of approaching horses filled her heart with joy.

We're so close, she thought as she quickened her pace.

Mickey pounced in front of them, his muscular body a wall, the mask taut over his skull face, as red as freshly spilt blood. But it was his pistol that brought Bram and Queen Georgina sliding to a halt – deformed by the glamour and aimed straight at the monarch's chest.

'Stop.' His voice was a judder. Mickey glared from beneath the scarlet mask, victory turning his black eyes into pools of swirling ink. 'It doesn't need a big speech. I'm just going to shoot you.' He smiled, revealing those horrible pointed teeth. His finger began to compress the trigger. 'Goodbye, Your Majesty.'

Everything seemed to slow.

The blast rang out around the moor, shaking the grass and the trees, causing birds to shriek from the leaves, and threatening to split Bram's head in two. The Queen screamed. And a single thought drove into Bram's skull: *I'm a Brigand, sworn to protect the one true queen.*

Bram dived in front of Georgina, using her own

body as a shield.

She waited for the pain of the bullet, for the red gush of blood from her chest, and for the screams of her friends and family as they realized she'd been hit.

But they never came.

Instead, Mickey's firing hand lurched to the side and he yelped in pain. The bullet flew into the Crooked Woods.

'What's happening?' Queen Georgina asked, pointing at Mickey.

Mickey began screaming and clawing at his face. No. Not his face. He was clawing at the magic mask. Smoke escaped in plumes from beneath the scarlet cloth and Bram realized that the mask was burning him. Mickey dropped to the ground, writhing and wailing in pain. 'It burns, it burns,' he screeched. 'Get it off me.'

Bram remembered all the times the mask had heated her pocket, the time it had singed poor Lena's fingers back at the glade. The mask really did know what it was doing. And it had acted when Mickey had threatened to shoot the Queen.

Finally wrenching the mask free, Mickey hurled it away and it landed at Bram's feet like a discarded rag. In an instant, his unnaturally large muscles and filed teeth vanished, and the monstrous highwayman was replaced by his usual self.

He staggered to his feet and groaned in pain. The skin around his eyes was blistered and pink, *burnt* by the mask, and his expression was fuelled with rage and pain. He looked less scary without the glamour, but he was still a big man, and right now, he looked ready to murder them.

Bram glanced towards her friends – they were halfway towards her, a row of determined faces atop a streak of blazing hooves. But Mickey wasn't about to wait. He ran at the Queen with his hands outstretched. A cry of fury blasted from his open mouth.

He's going to strangle her.

There was no time to debate, no time to feel small.

Seizing the mask, Bram shoved it to her face.

Whoosh.

Fizz.

She sprang between Mickey and Queen Georgina, once again offering herself as a human shield, and in pure desperation, pulled the stick gun from her apron string.

'Stop or I shoot,' she bellowed.

Much to her surprise, Mickey ground to a halt, his

fingers twitching just inches from the end of the stick-gun. Only his eyes moved, landing on the makeshift weapon in her hands.

'*That* is just a toy gun,' he said, though he didn't move.

Panic twisted through her body – just the smallest of movements and Mickey Ripheart could tear the sticks from the influence of the glamour. Then nothing would stop him.

And in that second, the past few days unfurled in Bram's memory: she had saved Ernest at the tavern, followed Agnes and Charlie to a hold-up, spied on the Rippers and found Grandpa. She cast her mind further back. She had survived the death of her beloved parents, and whilst grief had broken her, she had fixed herself with the strongest of glues: love, loyalty and adventure.

Ernest was right. She could do anything. And she could certainly stand in front of a nasty bully to protect her queen.

Forbidding her body from trembling, ordering her hand to stay straight, she said in her strongest voice, 'Oh, really. And you know it's just a toy gun for sure, do you? Because it looks pretty real to me.'

'I saw it at the cave.'

She puffed out her chest like a real highwayman. 'And you're absolutely sure I didn't have a real gun tucked in my apron before I put on the mask?'

Mickey faltered. 'Er – yes.'

Bram smiled. 'I'm happy to prove you wrong. All it takes is one bullet.'

'You're just a kid in a mask with a toy gun,' Mickey spat, yet still he didn't risk swiping at the fake weapon.

'Actually, I think you'll find I'm Diamond Jack,' Bram said softly. 'Notorious highwayman. Leader of the Brigands. Wanted in both town and country, protector of the one true queen, and most definitely armed and dangerous. And you, Mickey Ripheart, are surrounded.'

'What?' Mickey said.

Just then, a shot rang out, loud and clear.

Mickey jumped with fright, clutching at his chest. 'You shot me. You actually shot me.'

'That wasn't me,' Bram said, waving the stick in the air. 'How could it be? Toy guns don't fire bullets.' She laughed and pointed to her sister, who'd finally arrived, a smoking pistol aimed skyward.

'That was my other fearless granddaughter,'

Grandpa said as he leant out from behind Lena. 'And her gun is most definitely real.'

With a wicked grin, Lena pointed the gun straight at Mickey's head. 'Stand and deliver. Your magic or your life.'

CHAPTER 36

Bram watched as Grandpa and Lena marched Mickey Ripheart away, pistol pressed firmly between his shoulder blades. In the distance, the remaining guards had taken back their weapons and were securing the Rippers and the Princess Regent in the silver carriage, ready to take them to the palace dungeons. She spotted Ernest stroking Bertie beside the golden carriage. Everyone she loved was safe.

Queen Georgina turned to Bram, her face awash with tears and gratitude. 'Thank you, Diamond Jack, or whoever you may be. You saved my life.'

Not quite sure how to behave in front of the Queen now she no longer needed protecting, Bram knelt on one knee. 'Just doing my job, Your Majesty.'

Queen Georgina studied Bram's face. 'My father said the Brigands were not as they seemed, he even told me about the magic masks, but I always assumed they were' – she glanced upwards, searching the clouds for the right words – 'a fairy tale. That is, until now.' She reached towards Bram with delicate hands. 'May I?'

'Yes.' Bram stayed completely still and allowed Queen Georgina to gently pull the scarlet mask from her head.

A broad smile spread across the Queen's face. Bram had never seen her smile before; it was quite beautiful. 'It really was a toy gun,' she said with a giggle.

Bram nodded, tucking the roughly bound sticks back into her apron.

'And you are?' Georgina asked.

'Bramble, but everyone calls me Bram.'

The Queen smoothed down her dress and smiled. 'Well, Bram, what you did took a great deal of bravery. Thank you from the bottom of my heart.'

Warmth swelled in Bram's cheeks and she managed a bashful smile. 'You're welcome.'

'And these must be the other Brigands,' she said,

helping Bram to her feet and gesturing to Agnes-the-Blade and One-Shot Charlie as they looked down from their horses.

Charlie dismounted and bent into a deep bow. 'One-Shot Charlie, at your service.'

'Are you a child too?' she asked.

He nodded, then pulled the blue material free. The tall bearded highwayman blinked from existence, leaving behind an eleven-year-old boy in a baggy sweater, with cheeks full of freckles.

'Hello,' he said. 'It's me, Charlie. I know that you know that, but I thought I better say, just because I look so different.' His words trailed off and he wrinkled his nose.

Georgina smiled. 'Well, hello, Charlie.'

Her eyes moved on to Agnes-the-Blade and a sadness rippled across her face. 'I thought, perhaps . . .' Her voice fell beneath a muffled sob. 'Sorry. It's just, Bram said that my youngest sister was still alive, and foolishly I'd hoped—'

Bram realized that Georgina didn't recognize Agnes. Hardly surprising considering half of her face was hidden beneath a purple mask and she looked like a fully grown woman.

Smiling, Agnes blinked away a tear. 'Don't you recognize me, Georgie?'

The Queen covered her mouth with a hand and pulled a shaky breath through her fingers. 'Bea?' she whispered.

Agnes nodded, her face creasing with the effort of not crying. 'It's me, your sister, Beatrice.'

The Queen shook her head, sending her black hair flying from its bun, her features caught between disbelief and hope. 'No. No. Bea is dead. I simply can't believe—' Her voice dissolved in a sea of happy tears as Agnes leapt from her horse and removed the purple mask.

'Bea!' the Queen shouted.

'Georgie!' Agnes – now a bedraggled fifteen-year-old – ran to her sister with open arms. They stood for a moment, hugging and weeping. For a minute or two, they whispered to each other, and Bram assumed they were filling in the gaps from the past two years apart.

Stepping back, Queen Georgina wiped her eyes with a golden kerchief, which she then passed to Agnes. 'Why didn't you tell me you were alive?' she asked.

'I couldn't get to you,' Agnes replied, mopping her eyes. 'Lavinia had spies all around the palace and the hospital. At least I could protect the queendom from afar this way.' She waved the purple mask in the air.

Just then, one of the guards approached on horse-back. His dark hair was ruffled, and he had a cut on his cheek, but other than that, he looked unhurt. He smiled down at the Queen. 'Your Majesty. We need to get you to the palace before there's any more trouble.'

Queen Georgina studied the mask in Agnes's hand with a thoughtful look. 'Peter, do you know what these masks can do?'

The guard called Peter grimaced, perhaps unsure what answer he should give. Eventually he said, 'Why, yes, Your Majesty. They make people look scarier than they actually are. The Rippers were wearing them and it turned them into horrible things, and then the kids got them back and changed into ... highwaymen.'

Agnes released a huff of air. 'Kids, indeed.'

Peter looked at her and recognition flickered across his face. 'Is that ...'

'Hello, Peter,' Agnes said. 'Bet you don't recognize me without my tiara, do you?'

'Lady Beatrice?' he said, his voice tinged with delight.

Agnes grinned. 'Surprise.'

He jumped from his horse and knelt before her. 'Princess, welcome home.'

Agnes chuckled. 'Please don't bow, Peter. I live in a treehouse now.'

'How many people saw the masks working?' the Queen asked him.

Shrugging, Peter stood. 'The guards who didn't flee, we all saw the *magic*.' He hissed the last word as though it were something scary. 'There were about ten of us.'

'That's good to know, thank you, Peter.' The Queen shared a look of understanding with Agnes then cleared her throat. 'I think it's best if we burn the magic masks.'

'What?' Bram said, as Charlie shouted, 'No.'

Yet Agnes simply nodded. 'We can't have them falling into the wrong hands again, can we?'

Horrified, Bram swung her head between Queen Georgina, Agnes and the guard. She had only just learnt how to wear the mask, how to embrace that adventurous, confident part of herself, and now they were taking it away.

The mask in her hand grew warm. It was alive. Indeed, everything the mask had done had nudged her down this particular path so she could rescue the Queen. *The mask had a plan all along*, she thought.

'But you can't – you'll kill them,' Bram said, injustice burning her throat.

Agnes offered a kind smile. 'They're not living things, Bram. They're just enchanted pieces of cloth.'

'Magic is dead,' the Queen said. 'We have learnt how to live without it. If people find out about the magic masks, who knows what will happen. Witches, warlocks, sorcerers . . . they could come back. And we all know how that ends, don't we?'

Bram looked at Charlie, who was shaking his head and fighting back tears. What could they do? They served Queen Georgina. They couldn't go against her. So with heavy limbs and an aching heart, Bram bundled the scarlet mask to her lips, whispered the words, 'I'm sorry,' then handed it to the Queen.

The fire took quickly, built from dried pieces of wood scavenged from the edges of the Forest of Bells. Queen Georgina threw the magic masks upon the flames, and they blackened and curled within seconds. Bram stood between Grandpa and Lena, holding their hands and biting back the tears.

'It's for the best,' Grandpa said. 'There are always more people like the Rippers.'

Ernest snuggled into a whimpering Bertie. 'Bye, magic masks.'

Charlie turned his tear-streaked face into Agnes's side, and the guards watched on from behind the Queen.

Bram watched her scarlet mask fade into ashes and finally let the tears fall, yet as they fell, she realized they weren't just tears of loss. They were also tears of pride. She'd saved Grandpa, saved the Queen, made up with her sister and become Diamond Jack. Not bad for a twelve-year-old who worked in a shop.

The wind picked up, whipping the smoke across the moor. A cascade of chimes rang out from the Forest of Bells, setting the whole sky ringing with song.

Grandpa kissed the crown of her head. 'Time for a cuppa?'

CHAPTER 37

Things weren't so quiet in Mr Browning's Emporium of Strange and Magical Things. Not today. Lena was making sandwiches in the kitchen, Grandpa swept the floor, and Bram brushed Cornelius, the stag's head, whilst listening to Mr Wren and Mr Kipling's excited chatter. The coronation was that afternoon; Queen Georgina – the one true queen – would formally reclaim her throne, ending several miserable years of rule beneath the Princess Regent. The entire queendom was buzzing with excitement, as every townsperson and villager draped golden bunting, flags and streamers from lamp posts, door frames and trees in preparation for the street parties and barn dances that would stretch late into the night.

'Did you hear?' Mr Wren said, snaking a string of royal flags around the window display. 'When the Queen was held up on the moor, the Rippers were wearing *magic masks*.'

Mr Kipling balanced on a stool and chuckled, a ribbon of golden bunting clasped in his hand. 'You can't believe everything you read in the papers.'

'I suppose not,' Mr Wren replied. 'I mean, I read somewhere that the Brigands were just a bunch of kids.'

'Kids?' Mr Kipling said. 'Why not fairies? Or pixies?' He glanced at Bram. 'No offence, Bramble dear.'

'None taken,' she said, draping golden streamers from Cornelius's antlers.

Grandpa chimed in, trying to steer the conversation away from insulting children in case Lena heard. 'Marvellous news about Princess Beatrice, isn't it?'

'Apparently, she was one of the Brigands,' Mr Wren said, his voice incredulous. 'Turned up waving a pistol so she could defend the Queen.'

'A likely tale,' Mr Kipling said.

Yes, it is a likely tale, Bram thought. *She turned up waving a knife, not a pistol.*

'I suppose she had a magic mask too,' Grandpa said with a chuckle.

Mr Wren roared with laughter. 'Good one, Mr Browning.' He tapped his nose, trying to look like his job meant he knew more than most. 'Word is, the Queen burnt all the Rippers' masks anyway. Just so nobody would get any silly ideas.'

'Awful business, though,' Mr Kipling said. 'Apparently, Princess Beatrice was kidnapped by Lavinia's men years ago and suffered a blow to the head when escaping. She lost her memory entirely, poor lamb. She was living in the forest and hadn't a clue she was a princess.'

'However did such a helpless damsel survive?' Grandpa asked, his voice tinted with humour.

'Maybe a villager took her in, who knows?' Mr Kipling said, hopping from his stool. 'I'll tell you one thing for certain though – she wasn't a Brigand in an enchanted mask.'

'Couldn't agree more,' Mr Wren said, positioning the last royal flag.

Bram focused on Cornelius, so only he could see

the smile on her face.

Grandpa rested against his broom and nodded. 'Fancy not knowing you're a princess.'

'Hey,' Mr Wren said, laughing. 'Maybe I'm a princess too. Maybe we all are.'

Mr Kipling bowed, his white hair catching in the morning sun like a halo. 'Your Majesty.'

'Right,' Mr Wren said, dusting his hands together and admiring his handiwork. 'That's the emporium decorated, just in time for the street party this afternoon.'

'The villagers will love it,' Grandpa said. 'They've had such a tough time under Lavinia's rule, it's about time they had something to celebrate.'

'Things will improve for them now Queen Georgina is back in power,' Mr Wren said.

Bram thought about the many villages dotted through the Forest of Bells, about Betty and her baby, and her heart warmed. She couldn't wait to welcome them to their street.

Mr Kipling clapped his hands. 'I'm cooking a mountain of sausages, and Mrs Kipling has an assortment of cakes in the oven.'

'I've made my famous cookies,' Grandpa said.

Mr Wren held his belly. 'And I'll provide the service

of eating them all.'

After a round of polite titters, Mr Wren looked suddenly serious, his hand hovering on the door handle. 'Look, Mr Browning. I'm sorry we didn't manage to catch the villains who abducted you from the emporium the other day. I'm glad it's all sorted now.'

No thanks to you, Bram wanted to say, but instead, she just smiled. Not everyone was meant to be a hero, she decided, and Mr Wren had shown them real kindness over the past few days. He'd helped them put the shop back together and get things in order.

'Yes,' Grandpa said, returning to his sweeping. 'It's terrible when debt collectors get the wrong shop, isn't it? Apparently, they meant to visit an emporium of a similar name in the east of the city. They soon realized their mistake and released me.'

'Awful business,' Mr Kipling said. 'Just awful.'

'And so strange Bramble mistook them for the Rippers,' Mr Wren said.

Shrugging, Bram put an innocent expression on her face. 'I guess I'd seen too many wanted posters.'

Grandpa smiled at her. 'She's got a wonderful imagination. And I don't suppose it helped that Diamond Jack was spotted on our street. I think she had highwaymen on the brain.'

'I think we all did,' Mr Kipling said. 'At least we can rest easy now the Rippers are behind bars.'

'About time too,' Mr Wren said, before offering a cheery wave and leaving the shop.

Mr Kipling made to follow, but instead paused to study Bram. 'Funny business, seeing Diamond Jack run into the emporium like that.'

Bram felt her cheeks heat, but simply smiled. If she could fool Mickey Ripheart, she could certainly fool Mr Kipling. 'Maybe he was looking for his magic mask?' she said. 'It is an emporium for strange and magical things, after all.'

Mr Kipling laughed. 'Maybe he was, Bramble. Maybe he was.'

And with that, he left the shop.

Bram released a long sigh.

'Have they gone?' Lena called from the kitchen.

'Yes,' Grandpa replied. 'And just in time.' He checked his pocket watch. 'They'll be here any minute.'

Bram had just finished filling the teapot when the shop bell jangled.

Lena gasped. 'They're here.'

Bram dashed from the kitchen into the emporium to see Ernest talking excitedly to Grandpa whilst Bertie sniffed around the floor. She was always pleased to see her best friend and his loyal pup – and she was particularly pleased that his ma had finally ungrounded him for disappearing for two nights – but today, she was expecting another visitor.

'Bram,' Ernest said. 'I've got a better rhyme for you. Are you ready?'

'Rhyme?' Bram said, her brow furrowing.

He replied by leaping into a highwayman pose – legs apart, chest out, hands on hips – and launching into his ditty.

'Thanks for the pleasure, of stealing your treasure,
And please excuse my ramble,
Diamonds may shine, and look mighty fine,
but nothing cuts quite like Bramble.'

He jumped up and down on the spot, turning Bertie into a scurry of fur and excitement.

'What do you think?' he said. 'Do you like it? Brambles have thorns, you see—'

'It's great,' she replied, trying to hide her sadness. 'I'm just sorry I'll never get to say it.'

'What do you mean?' Ernest said, tilting his head at the exact same time as Bertie. 'That's why I wrote it. Brambles are better than Diamonds. You don't need the mask. You never did.'

Before Bram could answer, the bell rang again.

Two cloaked figures hurried into the shop from the busy street, bonnets pulled low and scarves worn high so their faces were barely visible.

'Quickly, into the back,' Grandpa said, ushering the mysterious figures into the kitchen.

'Chuck,' Bram called up the stairs. 'They're here.'

His voice drifted down the stairs. 'For real?'

'Yes, for real. Now come grab a sandwich before Ernest scoffs them all.'

Since moving into the flat above the emporium, Charlie had barely left his room. He was just so happy to have a warm comfortable bed, and a roof that didn't leak. Sleeping in a treehouse was only fun in the summer, he'd told Bram as he'd taken up post beneath his quilt.

Bounding down the stairs, two at a time, his red curls bouncing with every step, Charlie grabbed Bram's hand. 'Well, come on then. What are we waiting for?'

They stepped into the kitchen, where Queen Georgina and Princess Beatrice had already removed their bonnets and scarves, and were embracing Lena, Ernest and Grandpa.

'Aggy,' Charlie shouted as he dived in for a hug.

Bram curtseyed to the Queen, only to find herself swept into a firm embrace by the monarch.

'Oh, Bram,' Queen Georgina said. 'It's so lovely to see you again. I just couldn't have my coronation day without seeing you.' She looked at everyone else in the room. 'All of you.'

Before Bram could reply, Agnes had thrown her arms around her and lifted her off the ground. 'I've missed you, Bramble Browning.'

She grinned. 'And I've missed you, Agnes-the-Blade. Wait. Should I still call you Agnes? Or should I call you Bea? Or even, Princess?'

Agnes laughed, plopping her back down. 'You can call me Aggy.'

'What's it like living back at the palace?' Bram asked.

Agnes stuck out her tongue. 'It's OK, I guess. It's nice not to get rained on at night.'

'How are the horses?' she asked.

'Happy,' Agnes said. 'The palace stables are the lap of luxury. Dusty gets more apples than she can eat.'

Everyone squeezed around the table and Bram secretly fed Bertie a biscuit beneath the table.

'Tell me, Aggy,' Lena said, offering around the sandwiches, each stuffed with cold meats, cheeses and Grandpa's homemade pickles. 'Do you miss your mask? I still miss mine, and it's been a year since I've worn it now.' She giggled and held an embarrassed hand to her mouth, no doubt recalling her failed attempt back at the hideaway. 'Well, a year since it worked, at least.'

'I miss it terribly,' Agnes said, before biting into the sandwich. 'But not nearly as much as I miss my belt of blades.'

'Me too,' Charlie said, helping himself to three sandwiches. 'But I do like my new room and Mr Bramble's baking.'

Grandpa patted him on the back. 'You're starting school next week, aren't you, Chuck?'

Charlie nodded, his eyes wide with excitement. 'Lena and Bram said they'd help me catch up.'

The Queen ripped into her second sandwich. She

didn't eat at all how Bram expected – not a single delicate nibble of a crust or a raised pinkie. 'And what about you, Bram?' the Queen asked. 'Do you miss being Diamond Jack?'

Bram let the delicious taste of onions sautéed in malt vinegar fill her mouth as she slowly chewed. Did she miss the wind in her hair as she galloped after carriages, the holler of 'stand and deliver' ringing in her ears? Did she miss the confidence and swagger the glamour gifted? The feeling like she could do *anything*?

'Yes,' she said. 'I never thought I'd say this, but I do.'

Queen Georgina polished off her sandwich, then offered Agnes a side smile. 'Well, I suppose we better tell them.'

Agnes grinned. 'I suppose we should.'

'Ooh,' Ernest said, clapping his hands. 'Yes, do it now.'

Bertie scampered around his feet, his yips filling the kitchen.

The Queen leant forward. 'The Rippers are locked away, but there are other threats to the crown and to the people. Other highwaymen waiting to fill their places.'

'And Lavinia may be behind bars,' Agnes said. 'But she still has plenty of friends and supporters on the outside.'

Bram swallowed. 'Can the royal guard keep you safe?'

'There's only one group of people I truly trust,' she replied, opening her chatelaine bag and pulling from it three strips of cloth of different colours: purple, blue and scarlet. 'The Brigands.'

A squeal burst from Bram's mouth as her entire body surged with joy. 'The magic masks!'

Agnes laughed. 'You didn't really think the Queen would burn them, did you?'

Queen Georgina nodded. 'I just thought the Brigands should lay low for a while. You know how the guards like to talk. Much better they tell everyone the masks were burnt – some folk still believe in magic after all.'

'But I saw them burn,' Lena said.

'Me too,' Charlie said.

Ernest jumped from his chair, his face alight. 'I was in on it! I made fake masks from my rainbow coat back at the hideaway. Agnes thought I should, just in case. I said it was destined for better things, didn't I?'

'Oh, Ernest, you loved that coat,' Bram said.

'Yeah,' he said with a shrug. 'But I love highwaymen more.'

'Why didn't you tell me?' she said.

'I'm sorry,' he replied. 'It nearly killed me. You know how rubbish I am at keeping secrets. But it was for the one true queen.'

'Your reaction needed to look believable,' Queen Georgina said. 'Otherwise the guards wouldn't have fallen for it.'

'That was so clever, Ernest,' Bram said, hugging him.

Even Lena looked impressed.

With a broad smile on her face, Queen Georgina handed out the magic masks to their rightful owners. Charlie whooped, Agnes laughed, and within seconds two fully grown highwaymen were standing at the table, embracing whilst jumping up and down.

Bram sat with the mask on her lap, studying the sheen of the scarlet fabric and the intricate stitching. She let the material slide over her fingers, expecting the mask to demand to be worn. But there was no tingling and her arms remained firmly under her control. Perhaps it was because the Queen wasn't in danger any more. It was almost a disappointment. It was much easier when the mask was in charge, she decided. But then the mask always did have a way of knowing what was best – maybe she was supposed to take control now. Maybe the mask was telling her this.

She took a shaky breath.

So much had happened since she'd discovered it in the forbidden shed with Ernest. Most of it frightening and unpredictable. Could she really be Diamond Jack again?

'It's OK, dear heart,' Grandpa said. 'You don't have to put it on if you don't want to.'

'Brambles are better than Diamonds,' Ernest whispered, before chuckling softly. 'But Diamonds are pretty cool too. It's your choice now.'

Closing her eyes, Bram thought about everything she'd achieved. Rescuing Grandpa, saving the Queen, and facing Mickey Ripheart. *She* had done that. Bramble. Not Diamond Jack. Ernest was right, she didn't need the mask. It was just an illusion.

And yet she recalled the thrill of chasing down a carriage and that sense of freedom when she was riding Dusty as one of the Brigands. She imagined the adventures that lay ahead, the things that she could learn, the exhilaration of speeding across the moor, her locket bouncing free around her neck and her friends by her side. She imagined protecting the one true queen and the people who served her. She could do that as Diamond Jack.

Yes, the mask was just an illusion. But what a marvellous illusion it was.

'Stand and deliver,' she whispered. 'Your magic or your life.'

Then, with a quickening pulse and a shiver of anticipation, she lifted the mask to her face.

ACKNOWLEDGEMENTS

Firstly, I'd like to thank my wonderful family. Simon Rainbow, thank you so much for all your love and support, for your endless jokes and comfort, and of course, for lending me your surname. I love you to the moon and back. To my gorgeous kids, Ellie, Charlie and Fern, thank you for always making me smile. You are the centre of my world. Please stop arguing now!

To my darling parents, aka Gill and Len Waterworth, thank you for always being you. I couldn't ask for better parents and I love you both dearly. Remember how much I loved my nests when I was a kid? Well, I now have a little nest in my heart and I take it everywhere I go!

To my dear cousin, Lucy. This book is for you, even though you've never needed a magic mask to be your bravest self. Thank you for your giant brain and giant heart.

Thank you to everyone at Chicken House, especially my new editor, Shalu Vallepur. It's been a delight to work with you; thank you so much for getting behind my funny, magical tale and turning it into something shelf-worthy. To the rest of the team, Barry

Cunningham for his continued support, Rachel Leyshon, Emily and Esther, Rachel Hickman for all her work on the gorgeous cover, Jazz Bartlett Love and Ruth Hoey for their marketing know-how, Laura Myers for all her hard work in the later stages, and to Elinor Bagenal for her foreign rights wizardry.

Big thanks to Kesia Lupo, for helping me brainstorm in the earlier stages, and then later, for becoming my agent. Here's to many more new and exciting adventures! To the talented Isabelle Follath for the wonderful front cover, and to Sue Cook for her eagle-eyed editing skills.

To my fantastic friends, too many to list, but extra gratitude to Heather Thompson, Jenny Hargreaves, Natali Drake, Helen Spencer, Jenny Banham, Laura Williams, Catherine Field and Sam Lloyd, and to my sister, Helen Yates, and her family. Love you guys!

And finally, a big thank you to you, lovely reader. I really hope you've enjoyed this adventure. My advice – if you ever find a highwayman mask stashed in your Grandpa's forbidden shed, don't hesitate to put it on. Stand and deliver!